The Vessel
by S.E. Howard

Wicked House Publishing

No part of this publication may be reproduced, stored in a retrieval system, or transmitted in any way by any means, electronic, mechanical, photocopy, recording or otherwise without the prior permission of the author except as provided by USA copyright law.

This novel is a work of fiction. Names, descriptions, entities, and incidents included in the story are products of the author's imagination. Any resemblance to actual persons, events, and entities is entirely coincidental.

Cover design by Blaine Daigle
Interior Formatting by Duncan Ralston
ISBN: 978-1959798927

All rights reserved. Copyright © 2025 S.E. Howard

The Vessel

S.E. Howard

Chapter 1

I doubled my Ativan before leaving home this morning. Even so, by the time we pulled into the prison parking lot, I had dug my fingernails so deep into the passenger-side armrest that I had left indelible marks. All the way there, I'd tried the tricks I'd learned to ward off panic attacks: focus on my breathing, not deep or anything, just steady and slow; look at my arm, my hand, the pattern of stitches along the seam of my jeans; feel the denim beneath my fingertips; hear the drone of the car radio; be in the moment, not in the past.

Focus.

"Josh." Bree said my name softly, almost like a prayer, but still it startled me. She'd pulled into a parking space, turned off the car, and I hadn't even noticed. How long had I been sitting there, staring out the windshield with a thousand-yard stare?

"I'm alright," I mumbled, reaching for my seatbelt buckle. She draped her hand over mine. Her skin felt cold, but I jerked away like she'd scalded me. "I said I'm alright."

I got out of the car, my breath frosting around my face as I looked at the prison. A strong breeze made the flag in front of the main building flutter restlessly, its metallic rings clanging against the flagpole. The building itself looked almost medieval, with its tall, narrow windows, imposing stone façade, and towering battlements and parapets. Even though the sun was out, it seemed as if those rough-hewn walls swallowed the light the way a black hole would. Several steep flights of stairs ascended from the visitors' lot to the processing center.

I heard the car door shut. Damp asphalt crunched beneath Bree's shoes as she joined me.

"Why don't you wait in the car?" I said.

"Like hell. You're not going in there alone."

"I won't be. Rodriguez is meeting me at the visitor's check-in. And I don't want you going in this place."

The idea was almost like the thought of Traynor touching her. Which was pretty much unbearable.

"I don't want *you* going in there," she said.

"Yeah, but I have to."

"No, you don't." She looked up and now I could see tears welling in her eyes, making the whites turn all moist and pink, like peppermint candies that have been licked. "You don't have to do any of this."

"Yeah," I said again. "I do."

WHEN I WAS THIRTEEN, a man named Michael Traynor abducted me. His methods were crude, no online grooming or anything fancy like that. Rather, he saw me riding my bike one Saturday morning, figured I'd be an easy mark, and hit me with his car.

That part took some finesse, I guess, because he managed to tap the back wheel of my bicycle without actually running me over. It knocked me sideways, and I busted my knees and palms on the gravel shoulder of the road. In a flash, he stepped out of the car, the engine still running, and before I could recover, he clapped a rag over my mouth that he'd dunked in chloroform. From that point, I blacked out and I don't know how long it took for me to come back around. When I did, I found myself lying in bed in an unfamiliar house, my mouth covered with duct tape, hands bound, and a dead boy beneath a nearby window.

That's the last thing I remember until, nineteen days later, I noticed red and blue police lights flashing through that same window. My arms and legs felt weighed down with concrete blocks, my head filled with cobwebs and fog as I stumbled toward that flickering glow. It was nighttime, and I remember how cold it was when I stepped outside, enough to shock the breath from me. The police car was in the driveway next door, the neighbors shouting and shoving each other in their front yard, but their angry voices cut abruptly short as they all caught sight of me, barefoot, naked, and shivering.

"That kid looked like something out of a fucking horror movie," one of the neighbors later told a TV news crew. They beeped out the expletive, but you could still read the guy's lips. "Buck-ass naked, nothing but skin and bones. And that goddamn mask covering his head...!"

I'D MET Rodriguez three months ago on a cold night as I left work. I'd forgotten my gloves and had my hands shoved in my pockets, my shoulders hunched as I hurried across the parking lot. I had my earbuds in and was listening to "I'm Stranded" by the Saints. It's funny—no, ironic, I guess—how I can clearly recall little things like that.

I'd parked under a streetlamp and Rodriguez had pulled in beside me. At my approach, he stepped out of his car, little more than a silhouette standing in a pool of yellow light.

Puzzled, I slowed my stride, coming to a stop, and pulled my earbuds out.

"Hey, Josh," he said with a wave.

I work in a package warehouse because it means minimal human contact. At my own workstation, with my music on, I could tune out everything and everyone around me and focus solely on the tasks at hand. I didn't have to talk to anyone, didn't have to listen to any boring small talk or forced conversations. Nobody knew me, nor did they go out of their way to. I could clock in, work my shift, then clock out and leave, having said no more than a handful of words to anyone, and having had even less said to me.

In other words, it was heaven.

So when Rodriguez called out to me like we were friends, I knew we couldn't possibly be. I didn't have any.

"Who the fuck are you?" I asked.

"My name's John Rodriguez." He held up his badge and photo identification. "I'm a special agent with the FBI."

"What do you want?"

"Just to talk."

I snorted. "Talk to my lawyer then."

"C'mon, man, I've been waiting out here for an hour and it's cold as fuck. Just give me ten minutes." As if he was sweetening the deal, he added, "There's a Waffle House down the road. I'll buy you breakfast."

"I'm not hungry."

"Coffee, then. Come on. Ten minutes."

I didn't want to listen to anything he had to say, but I knew he'd never leave me alone. Cops and reporters never do. They're like a pack of rat terriers on a grizzled ham bone, relentless and ridiculous.

"Fine," I grumbled, shoving past him to unlock my door. "Ten minutes."

THE VESSEL

IT WASN'T the first time someone had managed to track me down. Every few years or so, on the anniversary of my escape, I'd have reporters sniffing around. And anytime a missing kid turned up rescued and alive somewhere, they'd want to interview me, as though I was some sort of de facto expert on the subject. My name still shows up on internet lists of missing children who'd made it home alive, alongside Jaycee Duggar, Elizabeth Smart, and those girls from Ohio. There are also plenty of Reddit threads and conspiracy theory sites still debating whether or not I was lying about the whole thing. Still, I tried my best to lay low and keep out of the public eye.

"You sure you're not hungry?" Rodriguez asked at the Waffle House entrance. I shook my head as he held the door open, letting me enter first. "It'd be my treat."

"No, thanks."

The diner was relatively empty, and we snagged a booth in the far corner. Through the window, traffic crawled along the highway in passing smears of white, yellow, and red-tinged light.

"You mind if I get something?" Rodriguez asked, rubbing his hands together as he perused the laminated menu. "I love this place, man. I haven't eaten here since college."

"Knock yourself out," I told him, and when a waitress approached the table, he went whole-hog, ordering the T-bone and eggs platter.

"Over-easy, please," he told the server as she poured him a cup of coffee.

"Anything for you, hon?" she asked, but I shook my head. She took the hint and walked away.

"You said you wanted to talk," I said, watching Rodriguez shake a pair of sugar packets before tearing them open to add to his coffee. "So, talk."

He pulled a manila envelope from an inner pocket of his coat. "I'm part of a multi-agency task force investigating other crimes Michael Traynor may have been involved with."

"Yeah, so?"

"So, I'm hoping you can help with that." He uncurled the twine holding the envelope closed, then pulled out a slim sheaf of papers: missing-person fliers, fanning them out across the table. "These are kids who went missing in this area around the same time as you did ten years ago. Do you recognize any of them?"

"No."

"C'mon," he said, with a patient smile. "You didn't even look. I read in a statement you made to police that you saw a dead boy at Michael Traynor's place when he first took you. Do you remember what he looked like?"

"No." As I pushed the fliers around, glancing through them, one caught my eye: a boy with blond hair and freckles, beaming toothily at the camera. *Avery Ormsby*, the name at the top of the page read.

"Are you sure?" Rodriguez asked.

I gave him a long look. "Are you deaf or stupid?"

He cocked his head like a Cocker Spaniel at a sharp sound. "What?"

"Or maybe you're both. You know my name, my face, where I work, the car I drive. Chances are, then, you also know I don't remember what happened when I was abducted. So, you're either deaf, or you're too stupid to know when to quit, because you keep asking me to do something that's impossible."

"Actually, it's not that you don't remember, but rather, you *can't*." Rodriguez's smile remained frat-boy-friendly. "You have localized dissociative amnesia, which is different from generalized memory loss, and often manifests with post-traumatic stress disorder, affecting the ability to recall important information of a painful or disturbing nature."

I blinked at him stupidly, caught off guard.

"However, I'm not asking you to do that," he continued. "I want you to tell me about something I know you *can* recall, because you've done it before, in that police statement years ago."

"I...I don't..." I sputtered, then scowled. "Who the hell are you?"

"I told you. I'm a special agent with the FBI." His smile widened. "I'm also a clinical psychologist."

"A fucking shrink. I should have known." I pushed myself toward the end of the bench. "We're done here."

Rodriguez caught me by the wrist. "I know how hard this—"

"No, you don't." I wrenched my hand loose with enough force to startle him. "You don't know a goddamn thing about me." I stood up, knocking the table with my hip hard enough to slosh his coffee. "Your ten minutes are up. Like I said, we're done."

AT THE PRISON, I emptied my pockets inside the visitors' processing center, then stepped through a metal detector.

"Did you drive yourself here?" Rodriguez asked.

I shook my head. "My sister brought me. She's waiting out in the parking lot."

They ran my shoes through an X-ray machine, much like at an airport terminal, then patted me down to make sure I wasn't hiding any illegal contraband. It felt like torture. Even though I tried to focus my attention elsewhere, keep myself distracted, it was all I could do not to shrink back or shove the prison guard away as he clapped his hands against my shoulders. He kept his touch light and swift, but even so, a sheen of anxious, clammy sweat broke out across my forehead, soaking beneath my arms as he worked his way toward my waist.

"Are you alright?" Rodriguez asked, shrugging back into his jacket, which he'd doffed during his own body search. He'd been watching me the whole time, gauging my reaction, probably trying to decide if I'd rabbit or not.

I nodded, even though I could hear my heart pounding inside my ears, could feel my chest heaving, on the verge of hyperventilation. Tiny pinpoints of light tap-danced across my line of sight, and I closed my eyes, pinching the bridge of my nose, struggling to will them away.

Focus.

"You need a minute?" he asked.

I bit back the urge to laugh because a minute wouldn't make a damn bit of difference one way or the other. It had been ten years already and I was still a fucking trainwreck.

"No," I said, hating him for dragging me out of the safe, quiet, comfortable burrow of anonymity I'd made for myself. "I'm fine. Let's just get this over with."

"YOU'RE RIGHT," Rodriguez remarked as he stood by my car, waiting for me after work again. "I don't know anything about you."

Two days had passed since he'd coaxed me into going to Waffle House with him. I wondered why it had taken him so long to try again.

"Fuck off," I growled as I sidestepped him.

"That's mostly your fault, though," he continued. "You don't talk to reporters as a rule. And you didn't testify during Traynor's trial."

"This is harassment. I'm going to call my attorney."

"He only got thirty years. With good behavior, he'll be eligible for parole in twelve. That makes, what? Another two left to go and he could possibly be free. Doesn't that piss you off, Josh?"

"Fuck off," I said again.

"That sentence is practically a slap on the wrist. Don't you want to—"

"I said *fuck off!* You think it's my fault Traynor didn't get locked up longer? Because I didn't testify? That wasn't my choice. They wouldn't let me. The prosecutors said I'd be an unreliable witness, that the jury wouldn't believe me because..."

My voice cracked, and I stood there, shaking with humiliated rage.

"I don't remember." I glared at Rodriguez, hating that goddamn pity in his eyes more than anything. "The son of a bitch drugged me the whole time. It's all a big fucking blank inside my head. I don't remember anything, and I don't want to. I can't help you, so stop asking already."

I reached for the driver's side door handle, but he caught my arm. When I recoiled, he must have seen it in my eyes, the wild sort of panic I always feel whenever someone touches me. Still with that sympathy twisting his brows, he raised his hands, as if in surrender.

"What happened to you wasn't your fault," he said.

"No shit." I tried to unlock the car door, but my hand shook so badly, I fumbled and dropped my keyring. Cussing under my breath, I stooped down to pick it up. "What, am I supposed to feel grateful now because you said that? You think it makes us friends?"

"Sure," he said. "If you want."

The response caught me off guard, but I managed a laugh. "Yeah, well, I don't. In fact, the only thing I want is for you to leave me the fuck alone."

I opened the car door, but he caught the frame with his hand.

"Avery Ormsby," he said. "He's a kid in one of the fliers I showed you the other night. I saw the way you reacted when you looked at it. You turned as white as a fucking ghost. It's him, isn't it? The dead boy from your police statement."

"I told you I don't—"

"That's who Traynor said it was, too. Only he claims he didn't kill him. If we can find Avery's body, we might be able to prove that he did. Then we can put Traynor away for life like the son of a bitch deserves. Not just for what he did to Avery, but to you, too."

"You...talked to Traynor?"

"Of course, I did. You think I like doing this, dredging this shit back up for you, freaking you out like this?"

I glared at him, curling my hands into fists, trying to stop them from shaking. "Then why are you?"

"Because he says he's done talking," Rodriguez said. "At least to me. If we want to go after him for murder, then we need to know where he buried the body. He's willing to help us, at least so he says. But only on one condition."

I knew what was coming next, but the words still hit me like a runaway bus blowing a red light and plowing through a crosswalk.

"He'll only talk to you."

Chapter 2

I watched through the thick glass pane as a guard led Michael Traynor into the room. At the sight of him, I felt my buttocks clench, my bladder threaten to give way, my breath tangle in the back of my throat. I caught myself against the dingy countertop as my vision swam out of focus. I felt dizzy and sick, grateful for the metal stool beneath my ass stopping me from crumpling to the floor.

Focus.

I curled my hands into fists, fingernails cutting into my palms. That pain, sharp and sudden, snapped my mind back to the present, and I watched him shuffle toward me with shackles around his ankles and wrists. He looked old now. His hair had turned gray, his face rounder, his jowls more pronounced. He'd gotten softer and wider through the shoulders and paunch. His jumpsuit was dark green, reserved for prisoners in protective custody, I'd been told. They kept him away from the general population; it seemed child rapists were the shit end of the totem pole in prison hierarchy, and he may as well have had a bulls-eye target painted on his back.

His face brightened when he saw me. He didn't smile, not

exactly, but his eyes grew wider and suddenly alight, a hint of color rising in his otherwise pale cheeks. When he sat across from me on the opposite side of the glass, his eyes bored into me. I couldn't move, frozen like a baby rabbit hiding in tall grass, the blades of an oncoming lawn mower bearing down.

He reached for the handset, drawing it to his face, then sat there for a moment, watching me. He nodded once, a mute directive or maybe an invitation, and my hand trembled as I reached for the receiver.

What was I doing? For the first time, the gravity of what was happening, what I had freely chosen, struck me. The air felt thick and heavy somehow; I gulped for breath, a hapless goldfish suffocating outside its bowl.

"Josh."

I'd forgotten how my name sounded when it came out of his mouth. My skin crawled as though maggots had burrowed just beneath the surface. I didn't say anything. I couldn't.

"My God, it's been so long," he said, his thin mouth stretching into a smile. "It's good to see you a—"

The whole room spun, and I dropped the receiver. Stumbling to my feet, I lurched across the room, seizing the first thing I could find—a plastic trash can beside the door—and vomiting into it. I braced myself against the wall as I retched, doubled over, and felt the snap of wind as the door flew open, cracking against the cinderblock wall.

"Josh!" I looked up and saw Rodriguez stood beside me, having rushed through the door, eyes wide with alarm. He made to reach for me, but stopped when I shook my head.

"I...I'm alright," I rasped.

"You sure?"

"Yeah." I spat the last ropy strand of bile from my lips. Rodriguez offered me a handkerchief, which I used to wipe my mouth.

"You want to stop?"

"No," I lied. I wanted to run out of that room, bolt down the front steps and beg Bree to take me home. If I did that, though, I knew I'd never get another chance. And neither would Rodriguez.

"Hey." He pointed to the corner of the room where a video camera was mounted in the ceiling.

"I'm going to be right next door, okay? I'll be able to hear and see everything that goes on. I've got your back."

He didn't leave until both Traynor and I were seated again. One of the guards brought me a bottle of water, and I mumbled in thanks as I unscrewed the cap and took a drink. Traynor watched the whole time.

It took a long, hesitant moment before I lifted the phone again, drawing it slowly to my ear.

"Are you okay?" he asked.

I nodded and he smiled at me, the overhead lights glinting in his eyes, as if he hovered on the verge of tears.

"I'm sorry, Josh," he said. "I didn't mean to upset you. It's just...I'm so happy to see you."

I sat there, mute. Rodriguez had given me some pointers on what to say, how to try and guide the conversation, but I couldn't remember a single one at the moment. My brain felt like it had been scraped loose and replaced with tapioca pudding.

"You look so different." Traynor leaned back from the counter, taking me in. "You're a man now. All grown up."

I didn't know how to respond, so mumbled an uneasy, "Thanks."

"I'm so excited. You can't imagine how much I've looked forward to this moment. All these years, I've thought about it —about you—hoping that you'd come..."

As I listened to him ramble on, I found myself mesmerized by how surreal this felt. Instead of a convicted pedophile and his erstwhile victim in a prison visitation room, we seemed more like old friends catching up in a coffee shop. It made me sick.

"Avery Ormsby," I said, cutting him off. "You told Agent Rodriguez you'd tell me where he's buried. That's the only reason I agreed to come." I gripped the handset hard and glared through the glass. "Tell me where he is, you fat, worthless fuck, so I can get the hell out of here and on with my life."

Traynor pressed his lips together and smiled. "Of course. Do you remember the place I took you to along Horsehead Lake in Virginia?"

I had no idea what he was talking about, no memory of that place whatsoever. "Is that where he is?"

"Near there, yes." That serpentine smile of his widened. "I can draw you a map if you'd like...?"

One of the guards brought him a sheet of paper and some crayons, and I realized they didn't trust him with anything like a pencil or pen because of the potential harm he could cause. He hunched over the page, clasping a crayon like a kindergartener would, his lips pursed as if he gave the drawing great thought and attention to detail. When he finished, he surrendered both the map and crayons back to the guard.

"Wait," he said as I rose to leave. "You don't remember, do you? Not about Horsehead Lake, or any of the rest of it? I read that you'd forgotten it all, some sort of amnesia, they said. Is it true?"

I was told he'd used Rohypnol on me, lacing my food and water, or shooting me up with it to keep me docile. He knew damn well what he'd done, the effects it had on me to this day, and to see him now, acting all innocent, like my memory loss was by my own choosing, made me bristle with rage.

"I remember enough." I slammed the receiver into its cradle.

"What happens next?" I asked Rodriguez when we debriefed in the main lobby.

"We get a search warrant for the property he told you about," he replied. "Then we bring in a forensics team, comb the area, and see what we can find. It's been ten years, and animals might have gotten to the body, scattered the remains. Hopefully something's left."

"Yeah," I said. No remains would mean no evidence. No evidence, no trial. No trial, no conviction. And no conviction meant Traynor would go free one day—one that grew closer by the minute.

"You did good in there," Rodriguez said. "Real good. I mean it."

"I'm just glad it's over with," I said. "Maybe now you'll leave me the fuck alone."

"Josh!" Despite the cold and drizzle, Bree had been pacing alongside the car while I'd gone into the prison. When I came back out, she ran across the parking lot to meet me. Her eyes were round and worried, and she reached out like she meant to hug me. "Are you alright?"

I raised my hand, warding her off. "I'm fine. Don't get in my face, okay? I've got puke breath."

I didn't miss the momentary flash of hurt in her eyes as I rebuffed her, but she tamped it down almost as quickly. "Are you okay?" she asked.

"I'm fine. I just threw up a little when I saw him. But it's okay now."

Even though she looked dubious, she didn't push the matter. The car ride home took two hours, most of which I spent with my head back and eyes closed. I wanted Bree to think I'd fallen asleep so she wouldn't ask me questions about what had happened, or what Traynor had said. Though it didn't stop Traynor's voice replaying inside my head, trapped inside my skull.

You don't remember, do you? Not about Horsehead Lake, or any of the rest of it?

The rest of it. What had he meant?

"You...uh, want to hang out a while?" Bree asked as she turned into the parking lot of my apartment complex. "We could watch movies or something, order pizza or Chinese."

"I can't. I have to work."

"Tonight? Come on, Josh. I don't think you should—"

"It's okay. It'll help get my mind off everything."

She didn't say anything, but her eyes held lingering concern. I leaned over and pressed my hand against her cheek. For some reason, it doesn't freak me out as much when I initiate touching. "Give me a rain check?" I asked.

"Alright Just be careful, alright? And tell Lucy I said hi."

"Bree says hi," I told Lucy as I walked into my apartment. She greeted me at the threshold, her tongue lolling, ass wiggling. I leaned down and hooked my fingers into the coarse fur of her scruff, scratching her favorite spot. Her heavy tail slapped a happy cadence against the entryway floor.

Her claws clicked against the hardwood as she followed me across the living room. I paused at the kitchen doorway, a post-it note stuck conspicuously in my line of sight:

5:30 PM – Took Lucy out, gave her more food. Come by later if you want. – P.

P stood for Paul, the closest thing I guess I have to a friend, a bartender at this place I go sometimes called Lupin's. The drinks are strong, the prices reasonable, plus it's within walking distance from my building. This works out well, since I can't always make it back to my apartment of my own volition, and more than once, he's had to drag my drunk ass home.

I'd told Bree I had to work that night, and it wasn't a lie, not a complete one anyway. I unbuttoned my shirt as I went to the bedroom, shrugged it off, then ducked into the bathroom to wash my face. Lucy hopped onto the bed and watched as I changed clothes. Her tail wagged again, rustling the unmade sheets as I scratched her head. I glanced at the clock. Ten minutes. I'd be cutting it close.

My apartment has two bedrooms, even though I live alone. The second one is smaller than the master suite, sparsely furnished with only a black sofa, armoire, computer desk with multiple screens, and a network of metal rigging and tripod stands positioning LED lights at various angles. I sat at the desk and opened a web browser, selecting my lone bookmarked site. The home page loaded: a simple black screen with the letters RLD in the middle. I entered my username and password.

Welcome, Easy Mark, the header on the next screen read. *Would you like to turn on your Red Light?*

I draped my hand against the mouse, moving the pointer toward a red button beneath this. *Yes,* I clicked.

Chapter 3

I discovered the Red Light District three years ago through Paul. He'd mentioned it in passing one night, an online community where viewers could watch live webcam models performing sex acts. Models work as little or as much as they'd like, attracting guests and subscribers to their channels by "turning on their Red Lights," an indication they were live and active online.

The first live session I ever watched was by a model named BJ Alex. I followed his stream for a while before working up the nerve to message him directly. He became a mentor of sorts, helping me get established, sharing tips on what viewers like, the most popular toys, best camera angles, and acts that get the biggest tips. Three years later, and I make a comfortable income as a "cam boy," more money than I make sorting packages. I keep the warehouse job, though, if only for the health insurance, and sock away as much money as I can in CDs, stocks, and my IRA.

"Hi, Gordon," I said, recognizing one of the usernames on my channel waiting list. I try to keep set hours for my livestreams: twice a week, Tuesdays and Thursdays, nine o'clock to one in the morning. Gordon was one of my first subscribers and remains one of my most faithful followers. If I had to guess, I'd say he's shelled out well over $15k to me through Red Light District over the past three years.

Hey, Mark, he typed, the only name he knew me by. He'd told me once he has a wife and three kids, lives somewhere up in Canada, and works as a distribution manager for a freight company. He traveled a lot as part of his job. I think he spent more time with me online than with his family in person.

"Where are you tonight?" I asked.

Denver, he replied, and when he asked if I'd ever been, I shook my head. *It's cold here,* he typed. *There's snow on the ground, about eighteen inches.*

A message popped up in the corner of my screen: *Subscriber Flesh_Gordon just tipped you 20 points!*

I laughed. "I haven't even started a game yet."

Thought I'd get a head start, Gordon replied, followed by an emoji: 😉

Leaning back in my chair, I smiled into the camera. "What do you have in mind?"

IT'S NOT like cam work is hard or anything. If my Red Light is on, anyone visiting the site can view my channel for free. They can buy packages of "points" and use these to "tip" me. Since that's how I make my money, I use a tiered system to encourage tipping: the more I earn, the more I do. Tip 10 points, I'll unbutton my shirt. 20 points, I'll take it off. 30 points, and I'll undo my fly. You get the picture.

Sometimes I let my viewers tell me what to do, where to touch myself, how fast or slow to go, all for a price. I also have interactive sex toys that viewers can pay tips to trigger, which means even more profit for me when I'm using them. That's where I make the most, to be honest, at least off my regulars. Gordon, for example, pays hand over fist to keep all my devices buzzing. He pays even more if I say his name when I climax.

I love watching you cum, Gordon typed hours later as I crumpled back against my chair, sweat-glossed and shuddering.

"I love letting you watch," I said. Then, after thanking all my guests for the wild ride and reminding them of my next show, I logged out, turning off my Red Light.

The site gets a percentage of the tips I make each session for providing the host platform. They also provide online security, masking my IP address, allowing me to block specific geographic regions if I want to, and encrypting my connection. What's left after their cut—around forty percent—is paid directly to me. The more popular a streamer becomes, the greater their percentage. BJ Alex makes sixty-five percent of his tips, but he's online nearly every day, sometimes eight to ten hours or more.

How the hell do you do it? I'd asked him once in a DM.

Viagra, he'd replied with an emoji that was both laughing and crying. *And a shit-ton of lube.*

Lucy waited for me outside in the hall, tail wagging, but I stumbled past her as I left the bedroom, naked. It occurred to me all I needed was a fucking gimp mask, and I could be the mirror image of the younger Josh who escaped Traynor that night ten years ago.

That kid looked like something out of a fucking horror movie, buck-ass naked, nothing but skin and bones...

This thought was too much, too soon after seeing him, and I rushed into the bathroom. Crashing to my knees, I hunched over the toilet bowl and vomited. When I finished, Lucy let out a whine from the doorway.

"I'm alright," I croaked as she padded over, then nuzzled

the side of my neck and ear, making me laugh. "Quit, silly dog. Your nose is cold."

Lucy followed me to the kitchen, watching with curious interest as I opened the fridge, fishing out a bottle of beer for myself and a slice of cheese for her. At the rustle of the plastic wrapper, her tail began swishing again in excitement. Mouth open, tongue drooping out, she waited with avid attention as I nudged the door closed with my hip, nestled the beer beneath my elbow, then unwrapped her treat.

"Good girl," I said, tossing the cheese in her direction. She caught it with a snap of her jaw, swallowing it whole. When I headed toward the living room, she trailed along behind me, sticking close as a shadow. She could always tell when something was wrong, when I felt anxious or distressed, no matter how hard I tried to hide it.

Lucy sat beside me on the couch, leaning against my leg, resting her chin on my knee.

"I told you I'm fine."

I twisted off the bottle cap, guzzling the beer in a few deep gulps. It probably wasn't the best choice to dump on my stomach so soon after puking, and with a grimace, I blew a sour belch against the back of my hand.

"What do you think?" I asked Lucy. "You want to go for a walk? I could use some fresh air."

She wagged her tail by way of response, and I chuckled.

"Sounds good to me, too."

LUPIN'S LIES about a half-block from my apartment. I've been told it was the neighborhood hub back in the day, a place where locals gathered and exchanged gossip over mugs of beer. Nowadays, like the neighborhood, it was pretty much a dive, a ratty little bar that served watered-down drinks to college kids haunting the nearby dormitories.

Its sole remaining appeal was that it remained open all night: 23-1/2 hours a day, a neon sign blinking in the window promised. Because that thirty-minute stretch of closing time encroached, the bar lay deserted when I stopped by. The chairs had already been stacked upside down on tables so the chipped tile floors could be mopped and swept. A "Caution: Wet Floor" sign had been propped near the entry, and I guided Lucy around it as we walked through the door.

"Hey, man," Paul said, looking puzzled but not particularly surprised. "You're out late."

"Or up early," I countered as he propped his push-broom against the wall.

"To-may-toe, to-mah-toe," he replied, approaching not me, but the dog. Leaning down, he tickled her jowls. "Hey, Lucy-lu. He dragged you out, too, huh? Is he out of beer at home or something?"

"Fuck off," I said, making him laugh. "Seriously, though. Thanks for letting Lucy out today."

"No problem. Glad I could help. You want a Carlsberg?"

I nodded, sliding onto a barstool and releasing Lucy. With the leash trailing behind her, she began circling the tables, probably hoping a random French fry had escaped Paul's housekeeping.

"Taps are already off," he said. "Is a bottle okay?"

I nodded as he leaned over, sliding back the brushed metal top of a cooler behind the bar. After digging around for a moment, he pulled out a bottle of beer. "Want a mug?" he asked, using the corner of a towel to twist the cap loose.

"No, thanks."

"So, what'd you get into earlier? You said you had to go out of town?"

"Yeah," I said, taking a drink. "Nothing special. Just something with my sister."

He's never mentioned my past, and I've sure as hell never volunteered or shared. I suspect he kind of knows—if not about the particulars, then at least the generalities—that something bad happened to me a long time ago. He also knows about my work on the cam site and isn't above joking that I owe him a fucking finder's fee for introducing me to it.

"Here," he said, pushing my spare key across the bar. "Before I forget."

"You can hang onto it, if you want."

His brows raised in surprise. "You sure?"

"Yeah, sure." I shrugged. "I probably should've given it to you way before now."

The corner of his mouth lifted in a smile, and he dug his key ring out of his other pocket, adding mine to his collection. "You're not getting a key to mine."

"Like I want to walk in on you getting busy with what's-her-name."

"Beth," he corrected with a laugh. "And she's out of town, went to Chicago or something like that." Inclining his head, he smiled. "If...you know, you want to come over."

He's polysexual, which he says means as long as it's good, he doesn't care who he fucks. Which, on occasion, includes me.

Tilting my head back, I swallowed another drink. "Only if you've got beer."

Chapter 4

I guess my parents did their best both during and after my abduction. After all, it's not like someone gives you a handbook on what to do, or how to act, or anything. My father is what you'd call a "man's man," a retired master sergeant in the Army who'd gone on to work for a couple of data analysis companies over the years. My mother is the quintessential, dutiful housewife. Finding themselves in the media spotlight during my disappearance, coupled with the stress of dealing with my abduction, must have been overwhelming. They'd also faced unflinching public scrutiny and judgment. I could look back through online news articles from that time and read comments ranging from sympathetic

Those poor people. Can't imagine what they're going through.

to the outright malicious

Who lets their kid ride their bike around on their own like that? I don't let mine get out of my sight. What did they expect?

and everything in between. After I returned, we joined the police chief, mayor, and governor in front of a barrage of clicking cameras, bright lights, and a forest of microphones as countless media outlets vied for photos of us. Looking back at them now, I see a shell-shocked boy still dazed from the lingering effects of drugs Traynor had pumped into him. My mother is beside me, looking frail, on the verge of weeping, while my father, stern-jawed and stoic, stands noticeably separate from us both.

In all the years since, nothing much has changed. Mom always regards me with a mixture of pity and sorrow, handling me with kid gloves, never certain what to say. The distance between me and Dad has only widened. He was never especially affectionate or demonstrative while I was growing up, but I think he's only hugged me once since my escape, a stiff and awkward embrace offered when the police had initially reunited us.

"It's good to have you back," he'd told me, as if I'd been away at summer camp.

I tried going back to school, if only because my parents had been convinced that if we just acted like everything was normal, that nothing had even happened, then eventually it would be. That delusion crumbled quickly, and I didn't even last a week at school. Everyone knew me, if only by name, and there'd been no escape from sideways glances, whispers, and snickers.

He's THAT kid...you know, the one who...

After my third fistfight in as many days, the school principal met with me and my parents.

"We know this is a period of readjustment for Josh," he said, sitting behind the desk in his office while my mom and I sat facing him. My dad stood behind us, arms folded across his chest, his face, like always, made of granite.

"We want to be as sensitive and accommodating as we can..." the principal continued, smiling at me in that sympathetic way most adults seemed to, including my teachers. And my mom.

"I'm sure this was all just a misunderstanding," she cut in, wringing her hands, and looking at me with a pleading sort of smile. "If Josh apologizes to the other boy, couldn't we just—"

"No," I said.

"Be quiet," Dad told me.

"I'm not apologizing," I said, glaring over my shoulder at him. "Because I'm not sorry. He was talking shit about me."

"Joshua David," Mom gasped.

"Don't use that kind of language in front of your mother," Dad said, bristling.

I jumped to my feet. "What would you call it, then? You know what that kid said? He asked if I liked getting fucked up the ass."

Mom uttered a low, warbling sound.

"Then he asked me if Traynor gave me a Dirty Sanchez when he was done, if he'd wiped his dick off on my face after—"

My father hit me with enough force to knock me sideways. I fell to the floor and when I looked up, I realized he was ashamed. Not by what I'd said, or even because I'd been fighting. He was ashamed of *me*, of what had happened to me, what Traynor had done, and the fact that everyone knew about it.

"Josh," Mom whimpered, hands outstretched. I slapped them away, recoiling from her.

"Don't touch me." I shoved past her, rushing for the door before I started to cry. "Don't ever touch me again!"

"Dude," I growled as I trudged out to my car after work. "I have a phone, you know. You can always call."

"Yeah," Rodriguez replied with an amiable smile, leaning

back against my driver's side door. "But then I'd miss getting to see that annoyed look on your face."

It had been over a week since I had last seen the FBI agent. I figured at some point I'd hear from him again, but hadn't expected to see him in person, especially not so soon. "What do you want now?"

"We've been searching the area Traynor told you about," he said, "excavating the site he marked on his map."

As he spoke, his expression grew solemn, that lackadaisical smile flatlining.

"Yeah?" I said, pushing my hands into my jacket pockets because it was cold outside and once again, I'd forgotten my gloves. "So?"

"So, we found something."

"That's good, right?"

Rodriguez hitched his shoulder in a shrug, then rubbed the back of his neck.

I suddenly had this weird sensation, as though I'd swallowed a live eel, and now it squirmed around inside of me. "That's what you wanted, right? To find Avery Ormsby's body?"

Rodriguez looked around, not as much as if he thought we might be overheard as he was weighing his options, thinking about what to say.

"You busy right now?" he asked. "Maybe there's someplace we could talk for a bit? I'd offer to buy at Waffle House again, but this probably calls for something stronger than coffee."

That eel in my gut began turning somersaults.

Chapter 5

I gave Rodriguez directions to Lupin's, vowing to meet him there once I got my dog. I went home, put Lucy on her leash, and walked to the bar, thinking about what Rodriguez had said—or more specifically, what he hadn't. Something was wrong. Things hadn't gone according to plan.

Had Traynor lied? I could believe that easily enough, and that might have been as good an explanation as any, except Rodriguez said they'd found something. His choice of words bothered me. If it wasn't Avery Ormsby's body, then what the hell was it?

Rodriguez had already tucked himself into a corner booth at the far end of the room by the time I arrived. The rest of the bar was relatively empty, with only a couple of guys perched on barstools nursing their drinks. Paul was working behind the bar and looked both surprised and puzzled to see me.

"I thought you worked tonight," he said by way of greeting. I usually don't come in unless I have the night off.

"I did. I'm...uh, meeting someone." Right about then, Rodriguez caught my eye from the back of the room and raised his hand. I nodded once in acknowledgement.

"Oh." Paul raised his brows appreciatively. "Nice."

"It's not like that."

"Oh." He already had a Carlsberg out for me, twisting off the cap.

I snatched the bottle. "Fuck off."

"They let you bring dogs in here?" Rodriguez asked, leaning out of the booth to offer Lucy his hand.

"We're kind of regulars," I explained. He had a bottle of Bud Light, and I looked at him in surprise as I slid into the booth. "Aren't you on duty or something?"

"Something," he agreed, lifting the bottle and taking a drink.

We sat facing each other in awkward silence, neither looking at the other. I let go of Lucy's leash, and she made her rounds of the bar, nose to the ground. Rodriguez sipped his beer, picking at the foil label on his bottle until he'd peeled back a ribbon-like strip, which he then began rolling into a wad between his fingertips.

"You going to talk, or what?" I asked finally.

He met my gaze. "What do you know about Horsehead Lake, that place in Virginia where Traynor sent us?"

I shook my head. "Nothing."

I'd never heard of it before, even though Traynor had spoken like he thought I had. It had left me curious enough to look it up online. I'd hoped that pictures of it might spark a memory, or at least a sense of familiarity, but they hadn't.

"It's about a four-hour drive from here," Rodriguez said. "Not exactly convenient. Only part of it runs across public land. The rest's all privately owned. Getting search warrants and forensics out there with all their gear was a shitshow."

"But...you found something, right? Avery Ormsby's body?"

"We found skeletal remains consistent with those of a male juvenile, approximately Ormsby's reported height when he went missing. There wasn't anything we could use to make a definitive identification, so we're running a DNA analysis. It could take six months to a year before we get any results back."

"A year?"

He nodded grimly. "Or longer. Depends on how backlogged the lab is."

I looked at the beer bottle in my hands. Traynor would be up for parole in less than two years. Avery Ormsby's body was the linchpin in Rodriguez's plan to pursue murder charges against him before then. If it took a year or more before they could even confirm the identity...

"It's cutting it close," Rodriguez said, as if reading my mind. "I know."

"Do you really need DNA proof? I mean, you found the remains where Traynor said you would. He said that's where he buried Avery Ormsby. Isn't that enough?"

"It'd be circumstantial evidence at best without DNA confirmation," he said. "That might not be enough to convince a jury. Especially since Traynor's still saying he didn't kill him."

"Then put me on the stand. I'll testify that I saw the body when Traynor took me, that he told me where to look, and... what?"

Rodriguez smiled at me in a weird, gentle way, like my middle-school principal had in his office that day when he'd met with me and my parents.

"What, goddamn it?" I snapped. "Are you going to tell me the jury won't believe me? You can't just—"

"There was another body."

I blinked. "What?"

"I'm not supposed to tell you this. It's part of an active investigation, information we haven't made public. But we found another body buried with the skeletal remains. This one was in a different state of decay—the active stage, we call it—which indicates it had been in the ground for a significantly shorter period of time. We're talking two, maybe three months."

"What?" I said again. It didn't make sense, not one goddamn bit.

"It's an adult male, we know that much. We're working on identifying him as fast as we can, but that still won't explain how he got there." He leaned across the table toward me. "I really need you to tell me anything you remember about that site. Anyone else who may have known where it is, anyone Traynor might have brought there besides you."

"I don't know." Hell, I didn't even remember Traynor taking *me* to Horsehead Lake."

"There's no way Traynor could have killed this man," Rodriguez said. "But there's a good chance he knows who did. He told them about that site, showed it to them, maybe. I need your help to figure out who that might be."

"I...I don't know. I don't remember."

"What if I helped you try?" he pressed. "With hypnotherapy, we could—"

"You mean hypnosis?" I shook my head. "No."

"It would just be you and me. I'm a licensed clinician and I know how to..."

"No."

"...help you recover only what you want, Josh. Only what makes you comfortable. We can even try a mild sedative to relax you if—"

"I said no!" I struck the tabletop with my fist hard enough to wobble our bottles and draw Paul's attention from the bar. "Look, I know you mean well, but I already told you. The drugs he gave me messed with my head. There's nothing for me to remember."

I expected him to argue, to try to change my mind, but instead, he leaned back and raised his hands in surrender. "Okay," he said.

"I want to help," I said, feeling like shit because he'd given up so easily. "It's not that I don't. I want to do anything I can to put Traynor away longer, but I just...I can't..."

"It's alright. It wasn't fair of me to ask. I'm sorry. You've been through hell. I've got no right to ask you to go through any of it again. I'll figure something out," he added with a weary smile. "Don't worry about it."

Before he could say more, his phone rang. He had it sitting on the table with the screen facing up, and even though he'd turned his ringer off, it still buzzed like a furious cicada at the incoming call. As the screen lit up, I saw the name on the caller ID: *Laurie*.

Rodriguez watched it ring, as if considering whether to answer. Then, with a sigh and an apologetic glance in my direction, he said, "You mind if I take this?"

I shook my head, and Rodriguez stepped away from the booth, his free hand cupping the bottom of the phone to muffle out the background noise.

"Hey," I heard him say. "Sorry. I know it's late. Something came up..."

His voice faded as he walked outside. Not waiting around, I slipped out of the booth and went to the bar.

"You chase him off already, or what?" Paul asked.

"Ha, ha," I said drily. "He had a phone call."

"Wife or girlfriend?"

"How the hell should I know? Give me another round, would you?"

Paul turned away, reaching into a nearby cooler, and someone stepped up to the bar beside me, uncomfortably close. I felt a hand fall against my shoulder, and I jerked away in reflexive surprise.

"Excuse me," a man said, tall and thin, in his mid to late forties, wearing wire-frame glasses and a black turtleneck. "Are you Mark?"

It was an innocent enough question, but it startled me all the same.

"Uh, sorry," I mumbled, averting my gaze. "Afraid not."

I pushed past him, heart pounding, adrenaline surging. *There are a million guys named Mark in the world,* I told myself as I ducked into the restroom. *Ten million, even, if not more. And the Red Light District masks my IP address and location. There's no way anyone could ever—*

The bathroom door swung open. The Steve Jobs wannabe who'd approached me at the bar walked in.

"Mark," he said again. "Hey, it's me, Miles."

My throat felt tight, and I swallowed hard. "I—I told you before, my name's not Mark."

There was no way he could know, no way he could have found out. I tried to cut around him, but he stuck his arm between us, blocking my path. Still smiling, he stepped closer. "You said you like to play games. Is this one of them?"

"I don't know what you're talking about." All at once, I was aware of my heartbeat, the cadence quickening, and could feel my breath tightening in my chest. "Get out of my way."

"I like games, too," the man, Miles, said in a low voice, reaching for me.

"D-don't...!" I flinched as his fingers brushed my cheek.

"I got a room at a hotel just down the block. We can play all night, if you want."

The pad of his thumb slid across my mouth, and a memory flashed through my mind: Traynor's thick fingers brushing against my lips like that, then pushing past, into my mouth, forcing my jaws apart. Shadows came swooping down, enveloping my line of sight like a hood falling over me. I felt like I was drowning, submerged in deep, dark waters, clawing desperately for the surface, struggling to breathe. Then I became aware of Rodriguez's voice calling my name and the world came back into bleary focus.

"Josh? Josh, look at me."

For some reason, I was sprawled on the floor in the bathroom at Lupin's, with Rodriguez squatting in front of me, cupping my face between his hands.

"It's alright," he said. "You're okay. Just breathe, Josh. Breathe."

But I couldn't. It felt like my throat had constricted to the circumference of a pinpoint, and my lungs burned with the desperate need for air. I pawed at Rodriguez's hands, frantic and terrified, wanting to push him away from me, yet beg him to help, but unable to force my voice to work.

"Breathe for me," Rodriguez said in a calm, gentle voice, inhaling deeply through his nose. "Come on. Big breath in. Everything's okay."

I drew in a ragged breath, then, as he exhaled, nodding to me in encouragement, I did the same. He smiled at this.

"Again," he coaxed, leading by example. "In through your nose...out through your mouth..."

We breathed together a third time, and that terrifying tightness in my chest seemed to ease. I could feel myself shaking, like I'd grabbed hold of a live electrical wire, my chest heaving with each ragged exhalation.

"Tell me three things you can see," Rodriguez said, which had to be the craziest fucking thing I'd ever heard, and the last thing I'd ever have expected. "Three things, Josh. Look around and tell me what you see."

"I...I see you," I croaked. "Your...annoying...fucking face."

He laughed at this. "Alright. What else?"

"There's...blood on the floor," I said, staring in bewildered surprise at the bright red streak across the battered porcelain tiles.

"You beat the shit out of that guy," Paul said, standing in the bathroom doorway, looking pale and shaken.

"What guy?" A sudden swell of anxiety came again. What the fuck had happened?

I like games, too. We can play all night, if you want.

"The one who hit on you at the bar," Paul said. "I turned around to get you a beer, and when I looked back, you were gone. Then I hear yelling coming from in here, and he ran out, blood all over his face, making for the front door like his ass was on fire."

I remembered now.

Are you Mark?

"Oh, God." I raised my hand, meaning to push my hair back from my face, then realized I had blood on my fingers, smeared across my knuckles.

"You ever see him before?" Rodriguez asked Paul, who shook his head. Looking back at me, he added, "Do you know who he was?"

"No," I said. It wasn't a lie. I hadn't recognized his face, but then again, I haven't seen a majority of my livestream viewers before. They're only usernames to me, lines of dialogue that appear on my screen.

"Do you think he's going to call the police?" Paul asked, and I felt a resurgence of panic. All at once, it hit me that this guy, Miles, could press charges, that I could be arrested. And if I was, and he'd met me through the Red Light District, he could tell them. Then it would become a matter of public record, a criminal complaint against me, and if the media ever got wind of it—the former pedophile's victim turned online sex worker—they'd have a field day. My parents would find out, and in all likelihood die of shock and shame. Everyone would find out, then no one would believe me—not

Rodriguez, or any prosecutor, judge, or jury, not even if I remembered seeing Traynor murder Avery Ormsby with his bare hands right in front of me.

I could feel my breath hitching, working toward hyperventilation again, but Rodriguez stopped me.

"Breathe," he said gently. "No one's calling the police. You hit him in self-defense. Besides, if any do show up..." He reached into his back pocket, pulling out his wallet. From the billfold section, he took out a business card, which he turned to hand to Paul. "Tell them to call me. I'll take care of it."

He offered his hand to me. I hesitated, but realized I still felt wobbly, and there was no way in hell I was getting off the floor without help. I clasped his hand, and felt the confident strength in his grip as he drew me to my feet.

"You alright?" he asked.

"Yeah."

"Your hand hurt?"

I looked down again. Beneath the bloodstain, my knuckles looked red and swollen. My fingers felt stiff and achy as I moved them.

"I'll get some ice," Paul said, ducking out the door.

"I'm really okay," I said to Rodriguez, still feeling embarrassed. "It was just a panic attack. That's all."

The corner of his mouth hooked in a wry smile. "Remind me never to hit on you."

I scowled, pushing past him as I limped toward the sink. "Fuck off."

Chapter 6

Rodriguez insisted on giving me a ride home, even though I said I was okay to walk.

"We don't know where that guy ran off to," he said. "I don't want him messing with you again."

I felt fairly confident that whoever that guy was, I'd probably traumatized him for life. Still, I gave in and accepted Rodriguez's offer.

"Hope you don't mind getting dog hair all over your back seat," I remarked, as Lucy bounded into his SUV. Going for a ride was her third all-time favorite thing to do after going for a walk and sniffing other dogs in the ass, so she parked herself squarely in the middle of the back seat, tail swishing against the upholstery, and looked around in eager anticipation.

"It's all good," he told me. "No one ever rides back there anyway."

Paul had put some ice in a plastic bag, then wrapped a towel around it for me. I pressed it against my hand as we drove toward my apartment building. The dull ache I'd felt in the bathroom had worsened into a deep, steady throb.

"Thank you," I mumbled. "For helping, I mean. Back at the bar."

"I didn't do much. Just got you to refocus." He glanced away from the road toward me. "You said it was a panic attack. Have you ever had one before?"

I nodded, feeling that shame spiral begin to wind up again. "It's been a long time. But I used to get them when I first came home."

"What do you think triggered it? Paul said that guy hit on you. Did he...did he try to—?"

"No. No, nothing like that. He just...touched my mouth. When he did, I...I thought of Traynor..."

That fragmented memory remained in my mind, like a bloated corpse that's bobbed to the surface from the muck-lined depths of a swamp.

"It's my fault," Rodriguez said. "I shouldn't have asked you about Horsehead Lake. I shouldn't have asked any of this of you. I'm sorry."

Despite his words, I knew I'd disappointed him. The same way I had disappointed the district attorney at Traynor's trial all those years ago. Rodriguez had been depending on me to remember, and in the end, I'd let him down.

We reached my building, and he pulled up in front, turning on his emergency flashers.

"I'll keep you updated on the investigation," he said. "But these things take time, so it might be a while before you hear from me. If you need anything in the meantime..." He shifted in his seat as he pulled his wallet from the back pocket of his jeans.

"That's my work number on the front," he said, pulling out another of his business cards. Flipping it over against the steering column, he fished a pen out from the center console and wrote on the back. "And this is my personal cell. Call me, okay? Anytime, day or night."

I held onto it, then cut him a glance. "Thanks."

Rodriguez cracked a smile. "Take care, Josh," he said. "I'll talk to you soon."

HE MUST NOT KNOW WHAT "SOON" meant. Two weeks passed, then three, all without any updates from Rodriguez. After a while, I stopped looking for him when I left work at night, no longer expecting to see him standing beneath the security light by my car. I kept his card under a magnet on my refrigerator but didn't add him to my list of contacts or anything. It's not like we were friends.

I kept an eye on the news, expecting to see at least a brief mention about the other body Rodriguez said they'd found, if not the suspected skeletal remains of Avery Ormsby. Nothing ever showed up, and I wondered if Rodriguez's team would keep it out of the press while the DNA confirmation remained pending.

Things returned to relative normalcy. I went to the gym, the grocery store, walked the dog, paid bills, and in the spaces between, slept, showered, and shit. On Mondays, Wednesdays, and Fridays, I worked my usual shift at the warehouse, and on Tuesdays and Thursdays, I did my livestreams. Saturdays, I generally reserved for private shows, one-on-one webcam sessions with Red Light subscribers, who pay $20 a minute—of which, I get my forty percent cut—to have me virtually to themselves.

"You know," I said, leaning toward my webcam. "You can change your screen name if you want."

A month had passed since the night I'd been approached in the bathroom at Lupin's, and although at first I'd been on guard, nothing had ever come of it, and I felt like I could relax back into a routine.

"After all," I continued, speaking to my one-on-one. "You're a bona fide subscriber now."

Usually, it's only high rollers who want a private session. Gordon booked sometimes, but because the cost racks up quickly and he's afraid his wife might notice, it's a once-in-a-blue-moon thing.

"I'm not very imaginative," my one-on-one replied. He'd digitally altered his voice, and even though he had the option of letting me see him through his webcam as we interacted, he kept it covered. Lots of guys did the same, which usually tells me they're straight (or pretending to be), and more than likely married.

"I don't know about that," I remarked with a laugh. "You've been keeping me pretty busy lately."

Guest_1226 was a relative newcomer to the District. Even though he had showed up in my waiting room several times over the past couple of weeks, it wasn't until two nights ago, Thursday, that I'd seen the checkmark by his screen name certifying him as a paid subscriber. My analytics dashboard on the District helps me keep track of who my better tippers are, and the types of things that tend to coax more money out of them. Work smarter, not harder, and all that bullshit. At any rate, Guest_1226 had been topping my list lately of not just good, but great tippers. This was the first one-on-one he'd requested, but even so, I'd gathered enough metrics on him to anticipate what he might be interested in seeing.

"Are you ready?" I asked him. I was giving him these first few minutes for free, since it was his first time and all.

"I don't know," he admitted with a nervous laugh.

"Relax," I said. "We're going to have fun." One by one, I held up a series of silicone toys so he could see them through the camera. "What do you want me to start with?"

The Vessel

LATER, I stood in my bathtub, my forehead pressed against the wall while the shower rained down in a hot, stinging spray against my skull.

Three hours, I thought, doing the math in my head, because that's how long that session had lasted. One hundred and eighty minutes.

At twenty dollars a minute, that's three thousand, six hundred dollars. And forty percent of that is...

I'd just made more in three hours than I made after taxes in two weeks at the warehouse. It was the most I'd ever made in a single stream, and I still couldn't quite believe it.

"Do you want to stop?" I'd rasped, an hour in the one-on-one. We'd just passed the $1,000 mark, and I told him as much, because there was no way in hell I wanted him to come back later and bitch to the admins to get a refund.

I'd moved to the couch by this point, switching to the webcam I have positioned directly above it, and as I spoke into that glinting black, unblinking eye, through the wireless earbuds I'd donned, I heard him growl in reply: "Do you?"

At that moment, the vibrator he'd selected earlier thrummed inside of me as he sent it a powerful jolt. I felt the sensation resonate through my groin, and arched my back off the couch cushions, uttering a low groan.

He'd been strange, but not in the normal, kinky way I'd grown accustomed to in these shows. He hadn't wanted to use the toys, at least not for a while, instead opting to have me undress first, then spread massage oil all over myself.

"Go slow," he'd told me, and that had seemed to be his theme for the evening, doing everything slowly, deliberately, from peeling off my clothes, to touching myself, even in the most mundane areas. He told me to take my time, and if I moved faster than he wanted, my hand straying farther than he intended, he'd stop me instantly. Even stranger, at one point, he told me to stop moving altogether, to simply lie there on the couch.

"What?" I asked with a laugh, feeling awkward and self-conscious. "Why?"

"I just want to look at you."

"What a freak," Paul remarked when I told him about it.

"They're all freaks," I replied, knocking back a shot of whiskey.

I'd finished showering, then headed over to Lupin's, figuring at that time of the morning, it'd be dead except for the chronic drunks or diehard regulars like me. I hadn't been going much otherwise, still unnerved by the bizarre encounter with Miles. If he'd been a customer of mine through the District, I hadn't recognized his face, or associated that name with any of my regular users. In any case, I didn't want to risk running into him again, even though, as Paul kept reassuring me, he hadn't been back since that night.

"You think it was him?" he asked me now. "The guy in your one-on-one."

"I don't know," I admitted. Though, I didn't think it was. Even online, I can get a pretty good gauge on people, I think, and I hadn't felt any of the off-putting sort of vibes I'd felt from Miles.

"It seems kind of coincidental, this guy showing up so soon after that night," Paul said. "Speaking of which, you never told me what you were doing here in the first place, meeting up with that FBI agent."

I blinked in surprise, wondering how he knew, then remembered Rodriguez had given Paul his business card. "You're not in some kind of trouble, are you?" he asked. "Because of your streaming, I mean."

"What?" I uttered a bark of laughter. "No. Why the hell would I be?"

"I don't know. Why the hell else would the FBI want to talk to you?"

I could tell he was worried, and wasn't going to leave the matter alone, so I sighed. "Look, it was about something that happened a long time ago. Ancient history. That guy, Rodriguez, just had some questions about it. That's all."

"And you don't think that's weird? The FBI wanting to meet with you on the exact same night some creeper shows up out of the blue, looking for Easy Mark."

I cast a wary glance over my shoulder. "Would you watch it? I never said he was looking for—"

"He called you Mark, right? What are the odds of that? Pretty fucking slim, if you ask me."

"There's no way anyone could find me," I said, and when he looked dubious at this, I doubled down. "There's not. They've got all kinds of security protocols in place to keep shit like that from happening."

"All I'm saying is it's fishy as hell, all that going down on the same night. Like a set-up or something."

"A set-up for what? I'm not doing anything illegal."

"If you're hooking up in real life, you are," Paul said pointedly.

"I'm not."

"Maybe the FBI thinks you are."

"Trust me, they've got much bigger fish to fry." Fishing my wallet from my back pocket, I thumbed out a twenty-dollar bill and tossed it onto the bar. "C'mon, Lucy."

She'd been stretched out on the floor nearby, but scrambled up at my beckon, shaking herself off, rattling the tags on her collar.

"You're leaving already?" Paul looked surprised, then contrite. "Don't be like that, man. You know I'm just trying to look out for you."

"Whatever." I leaned down to pick up Lucy's leash. "No one asked you to."

Chapter 7

On Sunday, I found Avery Ormsby's address online and drove out to see it, although I'm not sure why. He'd lived in an older, rundown neighborhood in a sketchy part of town, with vape shops, liquor stores, and pawnshops the most common landmarks aside from boarded-up houses. He'd grown up in a shabby bungalow framed by a front yard overgrown with weeds and a rusted chain-link fence sagging around the outer perimeter. A sign that read *No Trespassing* listed from the gate, alongside another: *Beware of Dog*. On the stoop, a lean tabby cat sat with its back leg cocked so it could lick its balls. I found myself slowing down to roll past, wondering if that cat belonged to Avery's family, if it had been his pet before he went missing. Cats can live for ten years or more, right?

The house's aluminum screen door banged open wide, startling the cat, which leaped down, darting across the yard. A woman tromped outside, barefooted, in blue jeans and a bright red hoodie. She appeared older than me, old enough to be my mother's age, and I wondered if she was Avery's mother. I sat in my car, immobilized, watching as she lit a cigarette, and took a long drag. When she exhaled the smoke in a swift, sharp stream, her gaze traveled across the street toward the intersection where my car sat, idling. Her eyes met mine for no longer than a second, but that was enough to make my heart jolt, my breath skitter to a gasping halt. I stepped on the gas, and the little four-cylinder engine in my car did its best impersonation of a roar as I drove away.

"Fuck," I whispered, clutching the steering wheel to the point where my knuckles blanched. "Fuck, fuck..."

What the hell had I been thinking? I didn't even know. It wasn't my place to seek Avery's mother out. What had I expected? That I'd walk up and introduce myself, tell her Avery and I had been kidnapped by the same sick fuck once upon a time, that I'd seen her son's corpse lying belly-down in his underpants, on the floor in Traynor's living room? That I'd found out where he was buried, so even if the police hadn't told her yet, they'd be coming soon, and wouldn't that be just great? One big happy fucking ending.

Gritting my teeth, I curled my hand into a fist and drove it against the steering wheel. "Fuck!"

My phone rang from the center console, startling me. I fumbled for it, knocked it onto the passenger-side floorboard, then had to pull over so I could lean down and grab it.

"Hey," Bree said brightly when I answered. "I'm heading out in a bit to do some laundry. Want to come along?"

I didn't, especially not at that moment, but I'd been putting off the inevitable for a while now, and my hamper at home was close to overflowing. My apartment building was older and had no washing machines on-site. Bree's building had some in the basement, but she says they're overpriced and never work, so she usually goes to a laundromat instead. It's cheaper for us both if we combine our loads, plus it gives us a chance to hang out a little, which we also hadn't done in a while. Not since the day she'd taken me to see Traynor.

"Where are you anyway?" Bree asked. "It sounds like you're driving."

I glanced in the rearview mirror and caught a glimpse of red: the woman from Avery Ormsby's porch had walked out into the street, watching me drive away.

Fuck.

"No place," I said, pulling away from the curb and driving again, widening the distance between me and the woman until she'd disappeared from view. "Let me run home and get my shit together."

BREE PICKED me up an hour or so later, and I shoved my clothes basket into the back seat of her Camry.

"Be more careful today," I growled at her as I sat in the passenger seat. "A pair of your undies got mixed in with my stuff last time. I don't need to know you wear that kind of shit."

"Poor baby," she laughed. "What, did your boyfriend get jealous or something? Think you picked up a side piece?"

"No, he put them on and modeled them for me. He rubbed his hairy balls all over the lace, and probably got lube stains from his ass on the thong."

"Ewww!" she cried, laughing again, slapping me. "You're disgusting."

She knew I was gay and that I didn't want Mom or Dad to find out. Not that it was any of their business anyway, but Mom would probably start to cry and want to know what she'd done wrong, if it was because of what Traynor did to me. And knowing Dad, he'd probably say—although not in so many words—that of course it was because of Traynor, that I was broken now, my insides and my mind all mixed up. Neither would listen nor otherwise care that it was something I'd thought about long before Traynor took me.

As we pulled out of the parking lot, Bree looked over at me, her expression hesitant.

"You doing okay?" she asked, and I nodded. "You sure? You look tired."

She knew about my livestreams, too. She didn't like that I did them, and cried when I'd first told her about it. But she never discouraged or disparaged me, only telling me time and again to be careful. I suspect she knew I'd been up late the night before with something related to this, but I kept the details to myself to spare her worry.

"Have you talked to that FBI agent anymore?" she asked.

"Rodriguez? No, not for a while now."

I've told my sister many things, but not that they found a second body buried with Avery Ormsby's remains. Rodriguez hadn't asked me to keep it on the down low or anything, but I kind of got the impression he meant for me to.

"Good." Bree sighed, like an uncomfortable load had just been lifted off her shoulders. Glancing at me, she smiled again. "I guess he doesn't need you anymore."

LIKE A DUMBASS, I didn't realize we weren't heading toward the usual laundromat, but once she turned onto an exit ramp heading for the freeway, I frowned.

"Where are you going?" I asked.

"Oh," she said, in a sing-song kind of way that instantly roused my suspicion. "I forgot. Mom called right after I talked to you."

Fuck.

"I told her we were doing laundry, and she said we should just go over there..."

Fuck, fuck.

"...save ourselves a few bucks." Bree turned to me, all big brown, innocent eyes. "You don't mind, right?"

BREATHE FOR ME.

I sat in Bree's car, on our parents' driveway, long after she'd gotten out and carried her laundry to the front porch. I listened to the tick of the engine as it cooled and felt tension ratcheting throughout my chest.

For some reason, Rodriguez came to mind, his calm voice, his gentle smile.

Come on. Big breath in. Everything's okay.

"Everything's okay," I whispered, reaching for the door handle.

"Josh," my mother exclaimed happily from the front doorway. "What a surprise!"

I knew that was bullshit, because Bree undoubtedly would have told her we'd be together that afternoon. But I played along anyway, managing a feeble laugh.

"Hey, Mom. Bree said I could throw some of my things in with hers..." I gave the basket in my hands a demonstrative jiggle.

"Of course. You can use our machines anytime. You don't have to wait for Bree."

Carrying my dirty clothes gave me a way to tactfully avoid her attempt to hug or kiss me. While Mom closed the door, I made my way toward the laundry room.

"Your dad's in the living room," she called after me, just as I breezed past the doorway and caught sight of him in my periphery, sitting in his rocker-recliner as always, facing the large-screen TV. "The Ravens game is on."

"Yeah," Bree said, all smiles as she intercepted me in the

kitchen, wrangling the basket from my grip. "Go sit down, Josh. I'll start the first load."

"I haven't sorted anything yet..." I began, glaring at her.

"That's okay," she replied, amping up the annoying good cheer just to piss me off. "I can do it."

"You want a beer, Josh?" Mom asked, clapping my shoulders lightly from behind, making me jerk in surprise. "We've got some cold in the fridge."

"Uh, yeah," I said, dancing clumsily away from her. "Thanks."

"I just put a roast in the oven. You guys are staying for dinner, right?"

"Oh, man, that sounds great," Bree gushed, popping back in the kitchen doorway. My basket of clothes was nowhere in sight, and instead, she held two bottles of beer which she thrust at me.

"Dad asked for one, too," she said with a shit-eating grin.

I hate you. I mouthed the words in her direction, but she whirled around and was off again, ignoring me.

"You look tired, honey," Mom said. "Are you feeling okay?"

"I-I'm fine," I said, not missing the flash of wounded sorrow in her eyes as I drew away from her touch. She never stops trying, never stops being hurt when I flinch. I've tried to make her understand, but still she persists.

"Are you hungry? I could fix you something if you—"

"I'm fine, Mom," I said again, leaning in to kiss her quickly on the cheek. "I promise."

"WASN'T EXPECTING to see you today," my father remarked as I walked into the living room, beers in hand.

"Uh, hey, Dad." I handed off a bottle to him. "Yeah. Bree just kind of sprang it on me."

I sat on the couch diagonally from him, and the usual awkward silence settled between us as we both directed our attention toward the oversized flat-screen. Here, a football game was already underway, into the second quarter from the looks of the scoreboard.

"The Bengals, huh?" I remarked, taking note of the opposing team. Dad murmured something in affirmation, and again, that oppressive and uncomfortable silence settled.

Being around my father kind of reminded me of walking outside on a humid afternoon in late August, that kind of suffocating, wet-wool sweater feeling that makes it difficult to sweat, let alone breathe. I took a sip of beer and pretended to watch the game.

"How are they doing so far this season?" I asked.

Dad made a harrumphing sound. "Too early to tell. They didn't play their starters in pre-season, so they're just now working into a rhythm."

I nodded, picking at a corner of the foil label on my bottle. As I peeled off a strip, I remembered Rodriguez doing the same thing that night we'd met up at Lupin's. A nervous habit, then, I wondered, just like I was doing now. Had I done something to make him feel that way?

"Where are you working these days?" Dad asked.

"Uh, still at the packaging warehouse," I replied, biting back the urge to add, *Just like the past five years.*

"Still on third shift?" he asked, without looking away from the TV.

"Yeah."

"I worry about you working those late hours," Mom said as she came into the living room carrying two large bowls of chips. "That has to be so hard on you."

"I'm fine, Mom. I get plenty of sleep. And anyway, it's better money with the shift differential."

"You're going to end up with back problems, moving all those heavy boxes around."

"I'm fine. Stop worrying."

"I'm your mother. That's my job," she said with a laugh, setting one of the bowls down on the coffee table in front of me. "You didn't say if you were hungry or not, but I figure you can't watch a ball game without beer and salty munchies, right?"

"Thanks." I leaned forward to snag a chip as she handed the other bowl to Dad.

As she left the room, I heard her talking with Bree in the hall. Mom always sounded different when she spoke with Bree, her voice lighter and more carefree, her tone less tentative and strained.

"I...uh..." Setting my beer on the coffee table, I stood. "I'm going to hit the head real quick."

Dad didn't avert his gaze from the TV. "Top of the stairs, third door on the right."

"Uh, yeah." I couldn't tell if he was joking around or being an asshole. "I remember the way."

Chapter 8

As I walked down the hall on the second floor, I paused at the door to my old bedroom. The furniture inside had belonged to me: twin bed, nightstand, chest of drawers, but no evidence of me remained apparent to distinguish them. The mattress had been stripped bare, and a couple of large cardboard boxes sat beside it. A thin layer of dust across the flat surface of my old bookcase shelves suggested Mom hadn't been in there to clean in some time. It smelled as empty as it felt inside, the air stagnant and stale.

When I first came home after the abduction, my room had looked untouched. Yet, even though everything in there, all the books, toys, games, electronics, and posters were mine, none of it had felt familiar. It was more like a museum exhibit, or a room in a historical home, the kind you tour through in Washington D.C. where velvet rope barriers prevent you from venturing close enough to touch anything.

I'd felt like a stranger in my own home, as much then as I did now, standing by the window looking out over the backyard. Truth be told, Mom and Dad had wanted their Josh back, the boy whose room they had so carefully preserved. I was the Josh who had come back instead.

My phone thrummed in my hip pocket, the ringer on silent. Puzzled, I pulled it out, expecting to see "Spam Risk" on my caller ID, considering anyone who might ordinarily call me out of the blue on a Sunday afternoon—namely Bree or Mom—was currently within shouting distance.

It was a Baltimore number, one I didn't recognize.

"Hello?"

"Josh? Hey, it's John Rodriguez."

Surprised, I shot a guilty look over my shoulder toward the bedroom doorway, making sure it was empty. "Oh, uh, hey," I said, peering out into the hall in case anyone had followed me upstairs. "How's it going, man? Haven't heard from you in a while."

"Yeah," he said, the word escaping him like a sigh. "I'm sorry about that. Are you busy right now?"

"Not really. I'm over at my folks' place, watching the Ravens game."

"Oh, man. Love the Ravens. You a football fan?"

"Not in the slightest," I said, and we laughed together.

"Maybe later, then? I was thinking we could meet up again."

"Yeah, sure. What time?"

"Eight o'clock? How about this place called Encanto? I'll text you the address."

"Sure. We can go now, though, if you want. It's no big thing. I—"

"No, you're with your family. I don't want to interrupt."

"You'd be doing me a favor. Trust me."

"Enjoy your visit," Rodriguez said with a chuckle. "I'll see you at eight."

ENCANTO WAS A MEXICAN RESTAURANT, the stereotypical kind with paintings of guys in sombreros leading burros in tow, or women in brightly colored skirts kneading handmade tortillas. The dry-erase standee propped at the main entrance promised a live mariachi band on Saturday nights, and an all-you-can-eat taco bar for lunches Monday through Friday.

I found Rodriguez in the furthest corner of the dining room, tucked into a booth, about halfway through a basket of chips, salsa, and a pitcher of margaritas when I arrived.

"Hey, man," he said, his cheeks high with tequila-infused color, his mouth stretched wide in that disarming grin he wielded so well. "Good to see you again."

Sliding out from the booth, he offered me his hand. For a moment, I froze, then forced myself to reach out, gritting my teeth, accepting the clasp.

"Good to see you, too," I said.

"I appreciate you coming out like this." We slipped into opposite sides of the booth. Raising his hand, Rodriguez flagged a nearby server. "You like margaritas? They've got the best this side of D.C. I'll split this pitcher with you."

"Sure," I said. "Sounds good."

After the server brought me a mug, Rodriguez filled it to the brim before topping off his own. "You been doing okay? That guy hasn't shown up anymore to hassle you?"

I shook my head. "Haven't seen him."

"Good." Rodriguez took another drink, then regarded me for a moment. "I'm sorry I haven't called. I had to go out of town unexpectedly. Another agent on the task force was handling the investigation while I was gone."

"It's okay," I said. Then, after an awkward pause: "I...hope everything's alright."

"My father died."

The words fell between us as if weighted down with lead sinkers.

"I...I'm sorry," I said finally.

He smiled wearily. "Thanks."

"Had he been sick?" I asked, unsure of what to do or say, feeling awkward and intrusive.

"No, it was a heart attack. He was a teacher at the university in El Paso. He didn't turn up for one of his classes, so a couple of students went by his office, looking for him. They found him on the floor."

"El Paso. In Texas, right?"

He nodded. "That's where I'm from, where I've been. I went home to help my mom with everything."

"I'm sorry. How are you doing? Are you...okay?"

I wished I could snatch the words back as soon as I'd said them. What the fuck was I thinking? Of course he wasn't okay. I could tell just by looking at him, the shadows under his eyes, the lines in his face, the lift to his brows. He was a wreck.

"I'm holding my own." He smiled again, but I could still see the sorrow in his eyes. He might have been better able to disguise it had it not been for the margaritas. "Sorry I left you hanging."

"You didn't. You told me it could take a while, the DNA tests and all that."

He nodded. "They've found some other things, too, at that site at Horsehead Lake. Evidence of an old burn pit that had been covered with dirt. Personal effects, like a watch, wedding band, part of a charred wallet."

He drained his glass dry before reaching for the pitcher.

"They also found two more bodies," he said, startling me. "Buried just like the others, with what looks like a child's remains at the bottom of the grave, and a fresher corpse at the top. An adult male. We think the items in the burn pit belonged to him."

Suddenly my mouth felt dry and tacky. I picked up my margarita and took a long swallow. "Who are they?" I asked, my voice small and damnably wavering. "Do you know?"

"There was part of an ID in what was left of the wallet, a Michigan driver's license."

"Michigan?"

"Yeah, someone named Antoine Sparks. We're trying to verify his last known movements through his credit card and financials, but it looks like he flew through Baltimore back in March. Had a hotel room in his name here in town, but he never checked out, never caught his connecting flight the following day. His family reported him missing two days later. We have another DNA analysis pending, and the coroner's going to try and match dental records for him in the meantime."

"And the other remains?"

"No idea. Just that they'd been there a whole lot longer and belonged to someone a whole lot younger than Sparks."

"Do you think..." I swallowed hard. "Was it Traynor?"

"I don't know. And even if it was, that wouldn't explain the second corpse in either of the graves. It's not like they were coincidentally found close by the skeletons. They were practically buried right on top of them. Somebody knew where those skeletons would be found. They chose those burial sites specifically."

When he topped off our mugs this time around, he emptied the pitcher. He motioned to our server to bring another, then glanced at me. "You do shots, man?"

"I've been known to, yeah."

The waitress brought a fresh pitcher of margaritas, then presented us with a pair of shot glasses, each filled treacherously to the brim with tequila. With a practiced ease, Rodriguez licked the side of his hand, the fleshy expanse between index finger and thumb joint, then sprinkled salt in the same area. Another lick, and he knocked back one of the shots, then pinched a wedge of lime between his teeth, sucking on the juice.

"The thing that gets me," he remarked, "is that burial spot, out in the middle of fucking nowhere. And I mean nowhere. We've had to use all-terrain vehicles to get equipment and supplies there. You're talking a logistical nightmare to try and haul human remains—adult or child—out that far into the backwoods, especially when you can dig a shallow grave just about anywhere. It doesn't make sense. But it seems we've got not one, but two killers using it for a dumpsite years apart from each other. It seems a safe enough bet that Traynor's one of them…"

"And let me guess…" I downed my first shot, wincing at the bite of tequila against the back of my throat. "You think I know who the other one is."

"I think you might, yeah. And that's why I want to take you out there tomorrow, show you the site. See if it triggers something in your memory."

I licked my hand again for any lingering salt, then downed the second shot, lime slice be damned. "I have to work."

"You can call in sick."

From across the room, our server caught my eye, and I held up the shot glass in one hand, and two fingers with the other. "Dos mas, por favor."

Rodriguez leaned back in his seat, brows raised. "You speak Spanish?"

"Some of the guys at the warehouse are from Mexico. I've picked up a little listening to them over the years."

I could tell he was patiently waiting for me to respond to his invitation. He was a hard guy to read. On one hand, he seemed outwardly likable and approachable enough. But I suspected that beneath that affable veneer lay someone more deliberate and calculating, as stony as my father could ever be, and then some.

What are you up to, Rodriguez? I wondered.

"What if we drive all that way, but it's all for nothing?" I asked. "What if I still don't remember?"

He flashed me a winning smile. "Then we'll try something else. But hey, I'm willing to give this a go if you are."

The server returned, presenting each of us with fresh shots. "Alright," I said, reaching for one. "What the hell. Let's see what happens."

Chapter 9

An hour or so later, after polishing off the fresh pitcher, plus several more shots, Rodriguez and I were both pleasantly shitfaced. I couldn't remember the last time I'd gone out drinking with someone other than Paul, and although I'd initially had my reservations, I had to admit, it wasn't horrible. Rodriguez told me stories about his father, how he'd coached his T-ball and little league teams once upon a time, and how his dad's love of the sport had rubbed off on him. Rodriguez had played baseball all the way through college, had even earned athletic scholarships because of his skills.

"I've still got the first mitt he ever gave me," he remarked. "I about wore it out back in the day, but I bet it's still got some use left in it..."

I found myself envious of the relationship he described. I'd never felt close to my own dad, wasn't even sure I liked the son of a bitch, never mind loved him. But I'd be lying if I said I'd never wished for something like that.

I'd taken an Uber to the restaurant that night to meet him, and after settling our tab, we agreed to share a ride home. While the driver waited in front of my building, Rodriguez helped me stumble inside. After all that tequila, I felt like I was trying to navigate the deck of a ship caught in a typhoon, but Rodriguez hooked an arm around me and, steady as she goes, guided me up the stairs to my apartment.

Lucy greeted us at the doorway. She must've remembered him from Lupin's, because she didn't even bother sniffing Rodriguez to make sure he was okay. Instead, she came right up to him, tail wagging and tongue lolling.

"I think your dog likes me," he said, bending down to scratch her head.

"Don't take it personal," I groused, slumping backwards against the wall. "She likes everyone. B'sides, she probably just has to piss."

"I can take her," he offered, but I shook my head.

"I'll do it..."

"You can barely hold your eyes open. Where do you keep her leash?"

As he ducked out with Lucy, I stood there in a daze, knees sagging. I wondered if I could comfortably spend the night against the wall, provided I could get my legs out from under me. Before I could figure out the exact logistics of this, Rodriguez returned with Lucy.

"Hey," he said quietly, putting his arm around me again. "You okay?"

I nodded, my eyelids drooping closed. "Never...better..."

I don't remember him leading me down the hallway, still in that same foggy sleepwalking state, but I remember the cool, soft press of my pillow beneath my cheek as I crumpled onto it.

"I'm going to scoot this trashcan over by the bed," Rodriguez told me. "In case you get sick, okay?"

I nodded. When he turned to go, I pawed for him, hooking him by the hand. "I'm sorry," I murmured.

"About what?"

"What happened to your dad."

He smiled softly. "Thanks, man. I'll pick you up around ten tomorrow, okay?"

I nodded, my fingers sliding limply from his arm.

"You need me to give you a wake-up call?" he asked.

"Fuck off," I grumbled. I closed my eyes for no more than a moment, or so I thought, but when I opened them again, the pale glare of sunshine forced me to squint. With a groan, I dragged a pillow over my head, if only to muffle the pounding in my skull. After a second or two, I realized it wasn't all in my mind.

"It's about time," Rodriguez said when I opened the front door. Then, with a laugh, he added, "Man, you look rough."

"It's your fucking fault."

Lucy bounded over, happier to see him than I ever remember her being for me, and when she jumped up to greet him, he caught her paws in his hands, waltzing in place with her.

"Hey, Lucy," he said with a smile. "You want me to take her out again while you get ready?"

"Please," I grumbled, shuffling back toward my bedroom. "Feed her, too, will you? She gets one scoop of the dry stuff mixed with one pouch of the wet. It's in the kitchen on the counter."

"It's ten o'clock," he called after me. "We need to hit the road soon, if we want to get back before nightfall."

"I'll be set by the time you get back."

I glanced across the hall. The door to the spare room was closed, but it occurred to me that Rodriguez had been in the apartment last night, in addition to today. I'd passed out before he left. Had he...?

I glanced behind me and saw Rodriguez leaving the apartment, holding onto Lucy's leash as she hopped excitedly around him. He shut the door behind him, and I looked again toward the spare room.

What if he'd looked inside last night? What if he'd seen…?

A sudden swell of alarm sliced through the lingering tequila fog in my brain, and I peered into the studio. I'd installed blackout blinds in there to cover the window and kept them closed at all times. I had to switch on the overhead light to look around, but from my perfunctory glance, nothing looked disturbed or out of place. Even so, it was obvious this wasn't just the typical home office or extra bedroom.

I imagined Rodriguez peeking in, then, curiosity roused, checking everything out, wondering what in the hell all the lighting rigs were for. If he'd looked inside the cabinet, he'd have seen my supplies: all the electronic toys plugged in and charging, the different props, oils, lubes, and costumes I used. Then there wouldn't be anything left to wonder; the purpose of the room would be pretty fucking apparent.

Shit. I never had people over except for Paul and Bree, both of whom knew about my livestreams. I'd never considered having anyone else in my apartment—hell, I didn't really *know* anyone else—so I'd never put any kind of barrier or lock on the studio door.

Shit. I'd be mortified if Rodriguez found out. *Shit, shit, shit, shit.*

Breathe for me.

I remembered his voice, his hands on my cheeks, steadying me, calming me.

Come on. Big breath in. Everything's okay.

That had become like a mantra to me over the past few weeks. Dragging in a long, deep breath, I backed out of the spare room and closed the door. With a heavy exhalation, I repeated to myself: *Everything's okay, everything's okay.*

I decided if he asked about it, I'd tell him. What the fuck, right? It's not like it's illegal. I'm a grown adult. I can do what I want in the privacy of my own home. And if he looked down on me for it, if he thought it was wrong or shameful or bad... well, then fuck him. It's my life.

By the time I changed clothes, brushed my teeth, and smoothed down my hair, Rodriguez had returned with Lucy. He puttered around in the kitchen, fixing her food like I'd instructed, and I heard the rapid-fire clicking of her claws on the linoleum as she danced around in eager anticipation.

"There's a good girl," he said, setting down the plastic bowl with her breakfast. Glancing up, he saw me and smiled. "Hey, looking a little more human now at least."

I felt another shiver of panic, thinking again how he may have looked in the spare room, discovered my dirty secret. I tried to remind myself that I didn't care, didn't give a shit what anyone thought of me, including Rodriguez, but then it occurred to me that this wasn't exactly true. At least not anymore, not for Rodriguez.

"You, uh, ready, then?" I asked.

"Yep. You might want to grab some hiking boots, if you've got any. Either that, or shoes with good treads. We'll have to do some hiking once we get out there."

Before heading out of town, he swung through the drive-through at a fast-food restaurant and got us each a cup of coffee. He ordered a breakfast sandwich, and offered to get one for me, but the idea of greasy sausage and rubbery scrambled eggs squashed between two halves of a brick-hard biscuit made my digestive tract—having not forgiven my overindulgence in tequila the night before—gurgle in grim admonition.

"No, thanks," I told him. "I'm good with just coffee."

"Feel free to tilt the seat back, get some sleep," Rodriguez said after getting onto the interstate, heading south toward D.C. "It's going to take us a while to get there."

"I'm okay," I said, but as we drove along, the drone of the

engine, the gentle vibration through the SUV's chassis, and the warmth of sunshine filtering through the windshield soon made a liar out of me. It didn't help that when he turned on the radio, he had a Lana Del Rey playlist queued on Spotify, and the silken sound of her crooning, like cigarette smoke through rose petals, lulled me toward sleep.

"I really appreciate you listening last night," he said out of nowhere. I'd let my eyes fall closed, but snapped awake at the sound of his voice. Rodriguez took a sip of coffee, then glanced at me. "About my dad. Sorry I kind of rambled on about him."

"That's okay," I said, sitting up straighter, stretching slightly. "I didn't mind. I…uh, hope it helped a little."

He nodded, his expression growing wistful. "It did, yeah."

"You said he was a teacher?"

"Both my folks are. Dad was head of the political science department at UTEP. My mother's a professor of women's studies there."

"UTEP?"

"University of Texas at El Paso."

"That's where you said you're from, right? How'd you end up in Maryland?"

Rodriguez shrugged. "I got my undergraduate degree from UTEP, then went to Marymount in D.C. for grad work. Wound up landing an internship at the FBI's Behavioral Analyst division. The rest, as they say, is history." He took another sip of coffee. "How about you?"

"I was born and raised here." I gazed out the passenger window, watching the landscape fly by. "Probably going to die here, too. It's not like I have much by way of future prospects. School and me…didn't work out so hot."

"How come?"

"I tried to go when I first came back…after Traynor. But everyone knew what'd happened. Nobody wanted to be around me because of it. Some kids thought I was just making it up, my amnesia. Some of my teachers thought so too. And I'd get teased, get into fights." I shrugged. "I just got sick of everyone knowing. Whispering shit about me. So, I quit."

"You never graduated high school?"

I shook my head. "Got my GED when I turned sixteen, and a work permit, too, so I could get a job full-time. I moved in with Bree after that. She's older than me, so she already had her own place."

"Your parents didn't object?"

"They were probably glad to see me go by that point. They never knew what to do with me after I came home. Especially my dad. We never really got along, but around that time, it got pretty bad."

"Your counselor didn't help?"

"I didn't have one. I mean, for a while I did, when I first came home. The district attorney set me up before the trial. I guess he thought I was lying about not remembering anything. The shrink he found is the one who first diagnosed me with that disassociated amnesia shit."

"Dissociative," Rodriguez corrected.

"Whatever. The shrink also said because Traynor had drugged me, even if I did remember something, it wouldn't be reliable. That's why they wouldn't let me testify. They said Traynor's lawyers would crucify me on the stand. Their exact words."

"Why didn't you get counseling after the trial?"

"My dad. He said the court shrink didn't do shit, and with Traynor in jail, he wanted us to move on with life. So, we did."

Rodriguez looked troubled at this. "You've never thought you needed it?"

"Never really thought about it."

We drove in silence after that, and again, I started nodding off. I'd knocked back a couple of ibuprofen before leaving my apartment, and at long last, it felt like they started to kick in, the miserable, hungover pounding in my head beginning to subside. I closed my eyes, tipping my head to the side this time, resting my temple against the cool window glass, my cheek against the shoulder strap of my seat belt. Before I knew it, I was asleep, and didn't wake again until the truck slowed down along the slope of an exit ramp several hours later.

Blinking stupidly, I lifted my head, groggy and disoriented. The muscles in my neck ached, and I reached up, rubbing at the crick. "Are we there?"

"Not quite," Rodriguez replied. "About another hour or so."

My mouth felt dry and sticky, like I'd been sleeping with it hanging ajar. I picked up my coffee and took a drink, grimacing when I found it was cold.

"I'm going to stop for gas before we get too far off the main roads," Rodriguez said. "Once we're in the back country, there's nothing out there for miles."

I nodded as he pulled into a gas station off the exit. "Think I'll get something to drink," I mumbled, reaching down to unbuckle my seat belt. "You want anything?"

"Grab me a Coke? Let me give you some money."

"I got it." I stepped outside. It felt heavenly to stretch my legs, and I paused for a moment, pressing my hands against my lower back and arching my spine.

Once inside the store, I hit the bathroom and took a piss, then grabbed sodas along with a few snacks for the road. When I returned, I found him standing toward the back of the truck, holding his cell phone tight against his ear. He paced back and forth, his posture tense, his brows narrowed. I couldn't make out what he was saying, but it didn't take a genius to figure out he was arguing with someone. Feeling intrusive, I climbed back into the SUV and waited for him in the passenger seat.

"Sorry about that," he said several minutes later as he got back behind the wheel.

"Everything okay?" I asked, offering him one of the bottles of Coke.

"Yeah. Just had to get a hold of that other agent I told you about, the one who took the lead while I went home to Texas." He twisted off the cap, then took a drink. "She's out of the Winchester, Virginia field office, and is going to meet us at the site."

Judging by the look on Rodriguez's face, he wasn't especially thrilled with this.

The rest of the trip took us along a winding series of two-lane highways and narrow backroads, each leading deeper and deeper into a densely forested terrain. At the height of autumn, I imagined the landscape would have been beautiful, with all the trees crowned in vibrant shades of orange, red, and gold. Now, most of the leaves had fallen, leaving behind barren limbs and a carpet of brown, the lackluster leftovers. We passed through a couple of scenic small towns, and by a scattering of isolated mobile homes and houses.

Just as I started to nod off again, Rodriguez turned off the rural route we'd been following, and the truck jostled and bounced. I heard the crunch and ricochet of gravel beneath us and lurched in my seat.

"Sorry," Rodriguez said. "It gets a little rough from here on out."

Earlier, he'd explained that there were less remote ways to access Horsehead Lake. Part of the area surrounding it was a public park, in fact, with a lodge, boat ramp, hiking trails, and camping. The site where they'd been excavating, however, was on the opposite shoreline, accessible only by crossing through several tracts of privately owned property.

"No paved roads," he'd told me. "Not even gravel ones in

some spots." With a sidelong smirk, he'd added, "You might want to pack some Dramamine."

After about thirty minutes, he turned again, this time onto a rutted dirt path with overgrown weeds on either side. I could hear them whispering against the outside of the passenger door as we rolled by. Another ten minutes in, and I caught a glimpse of something ahead of us through the trees, the dark walls and steeply pitched roof of a building of some sort. As it turned out, the dirt path was a crude driveway of sorts that came to an abrupt end in front of the building, which I soon realized was a large, abandoned house.

Once upon a time, it must have been magnificent. It stood three stories tall, one tiered atop the other like the graduated layers of a wedding cake. The faded exterior had once been white, but time and neglect had weathered the wood panels to dingy shades of gray. The windows on the first floor had been boarded up, but the panes on the upper levels still remarkably remained intact. The front porch spanned the entire main story but sagged in the middle as if rotten beneath. There was something stately yet sinister about the mansion, a feeling that left the hairs along my forearms and the nape of my neck stirring uneasily.

Like I'd seen it before.

I noticed a truck marked "Mobile Crime Scene" parked on the grounds ahead of us, along with a maroon SUV.

"Looks like she beat us here," Rodriguez remarked, putting the truck in park and cutting the engine.

"That other agent?"

"Yeah. Her name's Ellis." Reaching behind him, he pulled a windbreaker up from the backseat, dark blue with FBI in big yellow letters emblazoned across the back. "Word of warning," he added. "She's not real happy about me bringing you here today, so she might get a little shitty. Just let me handle it if she does, okay?"

"Uh, okay," I said, wondering why in the fuck he'd waited until now to tell me this.

We got out of the truck, and while Rodriguez shrugged into his jacket, I zipped the front of mine up. I don't know if it was because the sun had disappeared behind overcast clouds, or if the wind coming up from the lake was to blame, but it felt cold and damp outside, more than when we'd set off earlier.

"Hey, Ellis," Rodriguez said as the driver's door on the SUV swung open wide, and a woman hopped down from the cab. She wore a windbreaker identical to his, with blue jeans, and thick-soled hiking boots.

"Rodriguez," she said, tromping toward us. She was a petite woman, with a slender, athletic build, her dark blonde hair pulled back in a messy ponytail. Somewhere in her mid to late forties, she had fine lines framing the edges of her lips and eyes, and a rough-hewn complexion that suggested she'd spent too much time in a tanning bed during her youth. The corners of her mouth hitched down as she awarded me a perfunctory glance.

"This is Josh Finley," Rodriguez said. "Josh, Special Agent Laurie Ellis."

"Nice to meet you," I said, finding myself somewhat intimidated despite her small stature. Maybe it was only my imagination, but I got the impression she could kick my ass, and would enjoy doing so if given the opportunity.

"Mister Finley," she said coolly. Returning her attention to Rodriguez, she said, "Let's talk for a minute."

Rodriguez gave me a sheepish smile, then followed Ellis back toward her truck. I was alone, with the woods on one side, that creepy house on the other, and the unshakable sensation that all of this was somehow familiar. Although I couldn't hear exactly what they were saying, their voices quickly grew sharp enough to suggest this wasn't a pleasant conversation by the stretch of anyone's imagination, and probably one I shouldn't be privy to.

Pushing my hands into my jacket pockets, I walked toward the house. The ground underfoot felt soggy and soft from recent rainfall. There was no way to tell by looking just how long the house had stood empty, but judging by the state of its disrepair, it had been many years. The porch lay hidden beneath a blanket of leaves and tangles of fallen branches. The door, like the ground floor windows, had been covered with a thick panel of plywood, held in place by a heavy-duty hasp and padlock. Only a semicircular transom window remained visible, halo-like, above it.

Traynor had mentioned bringing me somewhere near here. Had it been this house? For the past ten years, I hadn't wanted to recall anything about my time with him, no matter how insignificant, but the idea that I knew this place felt like an itch inside my skull, or a word caught on the tip of my tongue, just out of memory's reach. I wanted to remember, tried to force myself, closing my eyes, pushing against that damn blank slate inside my mind that suddenly felt like a mile-high cinderblock wall, impassible and unyielding.

"Goddamn it," I muttered.

"Hey," I heard Rodriguez call from behind. He walked toward me while the other agent, Ellis, remained by her truck.

"You alright?" Rodriguez asked.

"Yeah. What is this place?"

"Don't know. It's private property, so we needed a warrant to be here." He cocked his head slightly. "Why? Do you recognize it?"

"No. Nothing like that." I'm not sure why I lied, but I'm sure Rodriguez could tell. Even so, he didn't push the matter, and instead hooked his thumb over his shoulder.

"So, look," he said, "there's been a change of plan. We're going to head out with Ellis to the other side of the lake."

I glanced back and found her watching us, her expression unreadable.

"Uh...okay. Is something wrong?"

"Nope," Rodriguez replied, and although he'd adopted his laissez-faire tone, I couldn't help but think he was faking it. "Nothing at all."

He was lying, too.

Chapter 10

During the summer months, the park was undoubtedly a popular place, with little cabins for rent along the shoreline, RV hookups and more primitive campsites, plus a sandy beachfront and boat launching ramp. Now, in late autumn, it lay deserted, the cabins shuttered for the season, the playground and picnic areas empty and forlorn, littered with fallen leaves and branches. Ellis's truck was the only other vehicle in the parking lot as Rodriguez pulled in. He hadn't said much during the ride, which only deepened my growing suspicion that whatever was going on was because of me.

"Do you recognize this place, Mr. Finley?" Ellis asked as I got out of the truck.

I looked around, wishing like hell that I did, that I felt even a little nagging hint of recognition, if only for Rodriguez's sake.

"No, ma'am."

"Ma'am. That's sweet." She said this with a smirk and a quick snort of laughter. "Agent Rodriguez has told me how this memory thing of yours works."

I bristled at the snide inflection she lent these words. "It *doesn't* work. I have amnesia about the time I was with Michael Traynor."

"Yes, I know. And he gave you Rohypnol, too, which interferes with the ability to form long-term memories. Which means anything that happened to you while you were under the drug's influence is irretrievably lost. Not even hypnosis would help. The trick is..."

She walked toward me as she spoke, draping her hand against my shoulder. When I drew back, she chuckled.

"I'm sorry," she said. "He told me about the touching thing, too. Anyway, as I was saying, the trick is, you weren't under the effects of Rohypnol the entire time you were with Traynor. Which technically means there should be some periods of your captivity that you might recall. In fact, we already know of one, as I'm sure Agent Rodriguez has mentioned to you."

"When I first woke up in Traynor's house," I supplied. "When I saw Avery Ormsby's body, yeah."

"Agent Rodriguez and I would like to see what else you might remember from that time. There's a chance you could recall additional details that might aid in our current investigation, give some clue, perhaps, as to the identity of the remains of the other child we've found so far."

"So far?" I turned to Rodriguez. "You're saying there might be more bodies?"

"We're excavating an additional site where cadaver dogs have potentially identified human remains," Ellis said. "Which is why I couldn't allow you onto the crime scene. Potential contamination. I'm sure you understand."

This last, she said with a thin, saccharin smile that didn't reach her dark, glinting eyes. I met her gaze evenly, growing annoyed.

"What is it you want from me?" I asked. "I took a day off work to come out here because Rodriguez said it might help your case. I don't appreciate you guys dicking around with my time."

Her eyes widened momentarily, then she laughed. "Of course. My apologies, Mr. Finley. What we'd like is for you to undergo hypnosis to see what else you can remember about the day Traynor took you."

"What?" It was my turn to laugh. "You mean right now? Do you want me to go lay down on that picnic table over there while Rodriguez waves a watch over my head?"

I wasn't annoyed now; I was pissed, and more so at Rodriguez. He'd lied to get me to go with him, tricked me into being there, knowing damn well how I felt about being hypnotized and that I didn't want to do it.

"Of course not," Ellis said. "There's a park lodge nearby. We've booked a block of rooms while our investigation here is ongoing. We can go there and—"

"Fuck that. I'm not doing it." Wheeling on Rodriguez, I snapped, "I told you already."

"Josh," he said, looking hurt. "Wait, I—"

"Did you think dragging me out here would force me to say yes? Fuck that—and fuck *you*." Yanking my phone out of my pocket, I stormed past him.

"I thought you wanted to help, Mr. Finley," Ellis called after me.

"Fuck you, too," I said without looking back, already opening my contacts so I could call Bree. It would take her hours to reach me, I knew, but I didn't give a shit. I'd rather stand on the side of the road in the damp cold than be around either Rodriguez or Ellis.

"Josh!" Rodriguez ran after me. "Come on, man, wait." He caught me by the arm, and I whirled around, wrenching myself free. "I didn't know. I'd never have brought you here if I did."

"Yeah, bullshit," I said.

"I wouldn't have. I'd never try to force you to do anything. Ellis set this up—set us both up."

"Bullshit. So, what...? All that last night about your dad, that was just to trick me into coming out here so you could hypnotize me?"

"No." He looked genuinely wounded. "No, Josh, I swear."

"Mr. Finley," Ellis called, remaining where I'd left her, with her arms folded across her chest, her ponytail flapping back and forth against her shoulder in the wind. "No one here's trying to trick you. We want your help."

"Josh," Rodriguez said in a quiet voice, drawing my gaze. "I swear to you I didn't know. If you want to leave, I'll take you home. We'll go right now."

"I can conduct the hypnosis session myself," Ellis continued. "I'm fully qualified to that end. Agent Rodriguez doesn't have to be involved at all."

I glared at him another moment, then over my shoulder again at her. "Forget it," I said. "I don't want you anywhere near me. Either Rodriguez does it—just me and him—or we're done."

"How does this work?" I asked Rodriguez.

When Ellis had mentioned a lodge, I expected rooms with rustic, wood-paneled walls, and taxidermy deer heads for décor. Instead, it looked like an ordinary hotel room, two double beds with white duvets and pillows, benign abstract art prints framed on the walls, with beige upholstered chairs, flat-screen TV, and Keurig coffee maker. I felt sure there was a camera in there somewhere, too, even though I couldn't see one conspicuously apparent. I'd told Ellis I'd do this if it was only me and Rodriguez, but she'd been too quick to agree, and I'm sure she was watching every move we made through a closed-circuit monitor in another room somewhere.

"You want me to lay down or something?" I asked.

"That's up to you," Rodriguez said. "If you're more comfortable sitting up, a chair's fine."

I was still pissed at him, despite his claims of innocence. Shrugging my jacket off, I tossed it on the end of the bed, then sat beside it.

"So, how does this work? You put me to sleep, then make me think I'm a chicken or something?"

He laughed. "No, nothing like that. You'll be awake the whole time. I can't make you do anything you don't want to."

"Too late," I growled.

He dragged a chair closer to the bed, then sat down to face me.

"I'm going to talk you through some breathing techniques," he said. "Just like we did before. And when you're in a relaxed state, I'll ask you questions about the day Traynor took you. It will be like you're watching a movie in your mind and telling me about it. You won't feel like any of it's happening again, or you're there in person. You'll be completely detached from it, describing to me only what you see."

"That doesn't sound so bad," I said, even though my heart rate had quickened, my rib cage tightening with anxiety.

"I'm not going to embarrass you," Rodriguez said gently. "Or hurt you, Josh. I won't ask about anything else but that day, and we can stop whenever you want. I give you my word."

I felt like quipping about how worthless that was, but looked at his face, his eyes, and bit the words back.

"Okay."

I reclined on the bed, putting my hands down to my sides as Rodriguez instructed. Glancing at him, I chuckled nervously. "Am I supposed to close my eyes?"

"You don't have to. If you want, you can look up at the ceiling, find a spot where you can rest your gaze."

I looked up at the popcorn ceiling overhead, the play of light and shadows across all the minute ridges and crests. There didn't seem to be any one place of particular noteworthiness or interest, and I laughed again.

"If you make me act like a chicken, I'm going to kick your ass," I told him.

"I'm not."

I raised my head long enough to shoot him a glower. "I'm still pissed at you, by the way."

Rodriguez nodded with a smile. "I know."

"Breathe in slowly through your nose as you count to seven in your mind." His voice had taken on that same gentle cadence, that comforting timbre I'd noticed at Lupin's on the night of my panic attack.

"Now hold that breath as you count down from four... three...two...and exhale through your mouth as you count down from eight...seven...six..."

We repeated this over and over until the sound of his voice felt like a ribbon of silk sliding across my mind. As my eyelids drooped closed, he changed tacks, asking me to focus on my face, then my neck and shoulders, working my way down, relaxing all my muscles in turn. Under any other circumstances, I probably would have called bullshit way before now, dismissing the whole idea. But something in Rodriguez's eyes, that strange but earnest promise he'd made to me

I'm not going to embarrass you, or hurt you...

made me feel like I could trust him, made me *want* to believe him.

By the time we reached my feet, I felt like room-temperature butter on a summer day, soft and malleable, on the verge of melting. Rodriguez fell silent for a moment, leaving me in that warm, dazed state.

"Let's talk about the day Traynor took you," he said. "Do you remember, Josh? Can you tell me about it?"

In my mind, it appeared so easily, so vivid and clear. My mom and Bree were fighting. I was eating a bowl of Cocoa Puffs, sitting in the living room and watching TV, but I could hear them in the kitchen.

"Why were they arguing?" Rodriguez asked.

Bree had planned to go with her friends that day. They were riding together to go see a concert that afternoon. Mom wanted her to take some books back to the library so they wouldn't be overdue. In the throes of teenage melodrama, Bree insisted she wouldn't have time. Mom put her foot down and told Bree she could take the books or miss the concert altogether, because she'd be spending the day in her room. Her choice. And Bree had gone stomping through the house in a rage, all righteously indignant and wailing: "You're ruining my life!"

She came into the living room, flopped down on the couch behind me, then after a moment, leaned forward to whisper.

"Hey, Josh. I'll give you ten dollars if you take the books to the library for me."

I agreed. I mean, shit, it was ten bucks, and I was thirteen years old. I could buy a used game for my PlayStation at GameStop for that. Bree told me not to let Mom know, swore me to secrecy, and for an extra five dollars, I agreed. She handed me a stack of books, then kept an eye out for Mom as I snuck into the garage to get my bike.

The books were hard to carry. I had to hold them against my right hip and maneuver my bike with one hand. More than once, I had to stop, because the books would fall from my grasp and hit the ground. Then I'd have to recollect them and set off again.

"Do you remember seeing Traynor's car?" Rodriguez asked.

I didn't. Not until he hit me. Even then, I didn't realize what had happened. I heard a sharp screech, then felt the bike shudder violently. I pitched sideways, landing hard, the books scattering as I scraped open the palms of my hands, my kneecaps on the asphalt. I banged the side of my head, too, and for a stunned moment, couldn't move.

I remember the sound of Traynor's car door opening, the scuff of his shoe soles as he hurried toward me.

"Oh, my God," I heard him exclaim in a breathless panic. "Holy Jesus, kid, are you alright? I'm so sorry. My foot slipped...!"

I raised my head, looking blearily over my shoulder. I saw a car less than three feet away, the mummified carcasses of insects killed mid-flight stuck to the grill.

"You're bleeding..." Traynor said, and I looked up at him, a large man with flushed cheeks and a greasy face. "Oh, Jesus, kid, here. Here, let me help you up."

He looked around, surveying the nearby houses and yards. When he returned his attention to me, he leaned down and I saw a glimpse of something white, a handkerchief in his hand.

"Let me help," he said again, pressing it over my mouth and nose. He hunkered over to hide his movements with his body, so at first glance no one would have seen or realized. The rag felt damp against my face, and I smelled something acrid, thick and pungent fumes that stripped my breath from me, burned the inside of my nose and throat. I tried to push him away, tell him to stop, but he only shoved the handkerchief against me harder.

"Let me help," he kept saying, his voice growing echoey

and faint, the world fading into dusky shadows as my consciousness ebbed.

"Are you alright?" Rodriguez asked me gently. "Do you want to stop?"

"No," I murmured. "I'm...alright..."

"What do you remember next?"

I could smell the leather of his car seats, feel the rumble of the engine beneath me, the soft jostle of the uneven road, and hear Traynor's voice as he talked on the phone.

"Who was he talking to?"

"I don't know." It felt like I had cotton balls plugged in my ears, or a pillow over my head. I couldn't make out any specific words. Except for one.

"Anathema?" Rodriguez repeated, puzzled.

I nodded. "Then he started to laugh."

I must have fallen asleep again, because I remember only being vaguely aware of a sudden light as Traynor opened the car door.

"It's alright," he said softly, leaning over, sliding his arms beneath me. I felt him pulling me out, lifting me up, and hung limply in his grasp as he cradled me against his chest. All I could see was the glare of sunlight and his face as he looked down at me. His skin looked shiny with sweat, and his lips stretched wide, his cheeks crimpling as he smiled at me.

"It's alright," he said again.

Once inside, he cut my clothes off. I roused again as he tugged at my T-shirt, then I heard the soft whisper of scissor blades, the rip of fabric. I tried to push him away, my hands floppy and clumsy.

"No, no," he said, catching my wrists. "None of that now."

That's when he bound my hands together, using a zip tie that he cinched too tight, enough so the plastic cut into my skin. He covered my mouth with a strip of duct tape, then pushed me onto my side. I felt his thick fingers paw beneath the elastic waistband of my sweatpants, pushing them down.

"Do you want to stop?" Rodriguez asked me.

"No," I said, but my voice sounded strange, strained somehow.

He began taking pictures of me, the flash on his phone firing repeatedly, washing over me with a stark glare that abruptly faded to shadows over and over. He turned me this way and that, positioning me on the bed in between shots, as if posing me.

When he finished, he stepped out of view, and I felt the mattress underneath me shift, the springs groaning in protest as he lay down behind me, close enough so I could feel the humid warmth of his body, smell the salty, pungent stink of his sweat. His breath huffed in my ear, growing sharper, and I could feel his hand between us, brushing against my ass. I knew what he was doing, but I didn't understand. I couldn't make sense of what was happening, and when I looked across the room, I saw a window. Drapes had been drawn to dampen the light, but enough seeped through to illuminate the shape of someone huddled on the floor, a boy no older than me, stripped down to his underpants. His body looked skeletal, the outlines of his collarbone and ribs all stark and apparent. His skin was ashen and riddled with cuts and bruises, large dark splotches against the pale canvas of his torso, arms, and legs. His eyes were open, and it took me a moment before I realized he wasn't blinking. Then I became aware of a pervasive odor in the room, like raw hamburger meat that had been left out on the countertop too long.

I didn't know his name then, but I do now: Avery Ormsby.

I didn't know his name, but I realized two things simultaneously, the thoughts breaking through the foggy haze of bewilderment and disbelief inside my mind. First, the boy by the window was dead. And second, whatever happened to him would likely happen to me, too.

"Did you see anything else, Josh?" Rodriguez asked. "Was anyone else there with you at Traynor's house that day?"

"No," I whispered.

It felt like hours that he lay behind me, his breathing coarse and ragged as he jerked himself off. When he finished, I felt something hot and wet splatter against the small of my back, and he trailed his fingertips through it, smearing it onto my skin, whispering words I couldn't quite make out.

Then he was gone. I felt the mattress shift again as he crawled out of bed. I heard the floorboards creak as he walked away, the squeal of the door hinges as he swung it shut behind him, the click of the latch falling home. Then another as he locked me inside.

I began to cry, drawing my bound hands up to my face, my knees toward my chest, but when I heard a soft rustle, then the floorboards groaning again, my eyes flew open with the sudden, terrified realization that maybe the man hadn't left at all. As my field of vision swam into bleary, tearful focus, I noticed something different about the room in front of me. The dead boy was gone, the floor beneath the window empty.

Had the man taken him away? I tried to push myself up to a seated position, then heard that strange rustling again, closer this time. Right in front of me.

I saw him, that dead boy from under the window. Only this time, he was crouched down beside the bed, peering at me. His eyes looked sunken, shadow-rimmed, and glassy. When he smiled at me, it was terrifying, like the hollow, empty smile of a department store mannequin, or a grim, life-sized doll.

With a strangled cry, I sat up on the lodge bed, snapping instantly out of the reverie Rodriguez had cast over me. At first, memory and reality seemed to overlap in my confused state, and I looked around wildly, expecting to see that zombie-like boy still hunkered down, watching me.

"Josh!" Rodriguez rushed toward me. "Hey, it's okay. You're okay. You're alright."

I stared at him, bewildered, disoriented, unable to catch my breath.

"Breathe for me. Just like before, in through your nose and out through your mouth."

He drew in a breath, and I hesitantly joined him. With a nod of encouragement, he inhaled again.

"That's it. Just breathe. You're okay."

"He...he was alive," I whispered.

"Breathe for me," Rodriguez coaxed.

"I saw him. I remember it now. He wasn't dead." Reaching out, I grabbed Rodriguez by the hand, clutching at him. "Avery Ormsby was still alive."

Chapter 11

"Here," Rodriguez said a short time later, offering me a can of soda. "They only had diet in the vending machine."

"That's okay." My hands trembled as I took it from him, then fumbled with the pull tab ring. At least thirty minutes had elapsed since the hypnosis session, but I hadn't been able to stop shaking.

"What happens now?" I asked.

"I need to go with Ellis. Back to the burial site, just for a little bit. Do you mind? You'll have to stay here until I get back..."

"You're not going to try again?" I asked, confused. I thought that would be first and foremost on his mind, getting back into my memories, revisiting that moment when I'd realized Avery was alive, finding out what happened next. "I told you what I saw. You believe me, don't you?"

"Yes. Of course, I do. But I don't think we should dig any deeper. Not right now, not today. It could traumatize you all over again, bringing up too much too fast."

"I'm fine," I insisted, tightening my grasp on the soda can

to disguise the tremors in my hands. "Let's do it. I want to know more. I'm ready."

He regarded me for a moment, then chuckled. "Two hours ago, when you heard the word 'hypnosis,' you were ready to kick my ass and hitchhike home."

"Yeah, well...That was before. And anyway, I thought this is what you wanted."

"It is. But I want to do it the right way."

He'd grabbed his windbreaker as he spoke, and slipped it on now, tugging the collar to situate it. "I'll be back in a few hours. Just hang out here, watch TV, order room service if you want." With a wink, he added, "It's on Uncle Sam's dime."

From the window, I watched Rodriguez and Ellis cross the parking lot and get into Ellis's truck. As he climbed into the passenger seat, Rodriguez looked back toward the lodge. He raised his hand in farewell, and, as he shut the door, I returned it.

Unsure what to do, I looked around the room. I sat on one of the beds, and reached for the TV remote. I flipped idly through the satellite channels for a few minutes, past an infomercial about a multivitamin supplement guaranteed to boost my sex life, and a movie about some kind of killer clown in a little cockeyed top hat. With a disgusted snort, I switched the TV off, then tossed the remote onto the far side of the bed.

Fuck this, I thought, getting up and snatching my jacket. Rodriguez had left behind a key card for me to use in case I left the room. I tucked it into my pocket before ducking out the door. The lodge rooms were arranged motel-style, all facing the exterior, and I followed the walkway toward the main building. The lobby was vacant except for displays of stuffed wildlife indigenous to the area, and furnishings upholstered with Native American-styled motifs. At the far end, I saw a gift shop and went inside. There were all kinds of books about Virginia history, postcards, coffee mugs, magnets, and toy versions of the taxidermy bears, beavers, and white-tailed deer on exhibit in the lobby. Out of curiosity, I paused in front of the book rack.

"Are you looking for anything in particular?" an older woman asked with a smile, stepping out from behind the cash register. She had a soft voice, short-cropped silver hair, and a nametag that read: *Suzanne, Volunteer.*

"Uh, actually, yes, ma'am, I am," I replied. "I was hoping there might be some information here about the lake. There's an old house on the other side. I saw it when I was down at the boat ramp earlier."

"The Brennus mansion," Suzanne said with a nod. "It used to be quite grand, as I understand it. It was built in the 1800s as a summer home for a prominent family."

"How long has it been empty?"

"Goodness, quite a while. I know after the original family sold it, it became a gentleman's social club for legislators and bigwigs from Washington. But that was years ago. I've heard they plan to renovate it eventually, turn it into a venue for weddings and things like that."

"Can you visit it? Go inside, I mean?"

"Oh, no." She chuckled. "It's all boarded up. It's hard to get to by car because it's all private roads, but people used to sneak over by boat. They must have caused all kinds of damage because there's been a lot of police up there recently. The FBI, too." This last, she added in a hush. "I don't know what happened, but you can't get within a half mile of it now."

Leaning past me, she perused the bookshelf, then pulled out a slim paperback with a glossy cover. "This might have more information about it," she said, offering it to me: *By the Shores of Horsehead Lake: A Brief History.*

"Thanks," I said, thumbing through it as she walked away. I came across a section of black-and-white images and paused, staring down at a ghostly image of the mansion. The windows and doors hadn't been boarded up, the grounds tended to and neatly manicured. A group of more than two dozen people—austere-faced men in suits and ties, women in satin evening gowns—stood in a formal sort of arrangement on the front steps and porch. *Corvus Society Summer Gala – July 29, 1934,* the caption read.

I felt my skin crawl with a strange sense of familiarity, just as I had when I'd stood in front of the mansion.

I paid for the book and brought it back to the room. Figuring Rodriguez would be gone a while, I kicked off my shoes, tossed my jacket over one of the chairs, and flopped back onto the bed to read. To my disappointment, there wasn't much more about the Brennus mansion besides the photograph I'd found, and roughly the same information the woman, Suzanne, had already shared with me.

The home had actually been built in 1849. The Brennus family had a long and illustrious history in business and politics, it seemed. Rather than having sold the estate, as Suzanne had mentioned, a descendant of the Brennus family, Allistair Brennus, had partnered with several other wealthy businessmen to form the Corvus Society, and established the mansion as their primary headquarters in 1887. The book stated that although the headquarters moved in the 1950s, the house and grounds remained the property of the Corvus Society, which was still in existence.

Curious, I set the book aside and used my phone to search online for more information. According to the main page of their website:

With 30 chapters nationwide, the Corvus Society is a traditional gathering of intellectual contemporaries, where integrity, decorum, civility, propriety, and social graces are the norm. Our membership boasts innovators, leaders, and influencers within business and political communities, and shares a time-honored dedication to philanthropy and fellowship.

Accompanying this crock of shit was a bunch of pictures of stuffy looking sitting rooms with wood-paneled walls, leather furniture, and mile-high bookshelves lined with tomes. Nothing about any of it felt familiar to me. Yet, why could I recall that old, abandoned house? All I could think of was that Traynor had brought me there at some point. After all, he'd directed us to the forest between the mansion and lakefront to find Avery's body.

Except Avery's not dead. Or at least, he hadn't been when I thought I'd seen his corpse. He must have died at some point, however, and maybe that's why Traynor kept insisting he hadn't killed him. Maybe he hadn't, not directly or willfully. The Avery I remember seeing had been in pitiful shape, emaciated and beaten. Maybe he'd died of natural causes after Traynor's abuse. Maybe Traynor had brought me along to Horsehead Lake to bury him.

But that still didn't explain why Traynor would have come this far, dumped a body in such a strange, remote place. Or why there was another child's remains discovered nearby—and possibly more, according to Ellis.

Not to mention who the hell had buried the fresher bodies on top of them.

I closed the internet browser, knowing I was wasting my time going down rabbit holes, and instead looked at the clock. It was getting late. There was no way we'd be home before dark, and by that point, poor Lucy would probably have pissed all over my apartment.

Hey, I texted Paul. *Can you take care of Lucy this afternoon for me? Had to go out of town. Looks like I won't be back before dark.*

While waiting for his reply, I stalked over to the window, looking out over the parking lot to see if Rodriguez was back yet. No sign of Ellis's truck.

This is bullshit, I thought, just as my phone dinged with a new inbound message.

Sure, Paul replied. *Will head that way in a bit.*

Thx, I texted, just as he sent another reply:

Everything ok?

All good, I told him, figuring I'd fill him in on the details later. Trying to explain to him by text where I was and why—never mind who I was with—would be too big a pain in the ass.

I didn't mean to fall asleep after that. I was still pretty hungover, to be perfectly honest, and when I stretched back out on the bed, I realized it was actually rather comfortable.

Before I knew it, I was dreaming of that house, the Brennus mansion, of walking toward the front steps again, just as I'd done earlier that afternoon. This time, however, I was a child again, naked and chilled to the bone. Yet my mind felt warm and fuzzy inside, like I'd been roused from a deep sleep, and still hadn't quite made the full transition to consciousness yet.

Someone held my hand, taller than me; from their wide build and stride, I could tell it was a man, and even though he was dressed all in black, with a mask covering his face, I somehow knew it was Traynor. The mask he wore was strange and frightening, panels of thick black leather stitched together, studded with silver rivets, with two circular eyeholes and an elongated beak covering his mouth and nose.

He looked down at me, and the skin around his eyes crimped, his smile hidden by the mask. He led me up the porch steps, where the front door of the mansion stood open as if we were expected. Warm light spilled out from the entryway, and beyond the threshold, I could see dozens of people gathered, men in tuxedos, women in elegantly beaded gowns and sparkling jewelry, all wearing bizarre bird masks like Traynor's.

I was led to a staircase with a grand, sweeping banister, gracefully curling up toward the second floor. All around us, I could hear murmured conversations and muffled laughter, as if this was a party of some sort, a celebration in progress.

Traynor brought me upstairs, where even more people had gathered. On the landing, they began approaching, stopping Traynor, shaking his hand, as if friends.

"Michael," a man said, stepping forward. A single blood-colored rose had been pinned to the lapel of his black tuxedo jacket, and the mask he wore had been painted to match. He struck a towering, elegant, imposing figure, and when Traynor caught sight of him, he seemed to diminish somehow, as if lowering his head and hunching his shoulders in deference.

"Let's see what you've brought us," said the man in the red mask, tucking his fingertips beneath the shelf of my chin and craning my head back.

"He's perfect," exclaimed a woman beside him. Her mask had been painted gold to match her dress, covered in glitter and sequins. "Just like in the pictures! Don't you think so, darling?"

"You've done well, Michael." Something about the man in the red mask terrified me. Maybe it was his voice, as deep and booming as the strike of a kettledrum, each syllable falling from his tongue like a block of granite. Or maybe it was his eyes, dark and glinting as he regarded me through the holes in his mask, a cold, detached appraisal.

"Are you pleased, then, sir?" Traynor asked. "Is he suitable for your needs?"

Without averting his gaze from me, the man uttered a low, rumbling laugh. "Please," he said to Traynor. "Call me Robert. And yes, Michael, he is quite suitable indeed."

Robert turned and led us through the crowd until we reached a large room. The blue paint on the walls was peeling, the plaster cracked and crumbling. Someone had stoked a fire in the derelict fireplace on the far wall, and the air felt thick, sticky from the heat.

"Here," Robert said to Traynor, lifting his hand in imperious beckon. "Bring the lamb this way. It's time to prepare."

Traynor led me forward, and as the crowd drew apart, I saw a bed with a rusted metal headboard and frame. Frightened and confused, I tried to pull away, dragging my feet to slow my gait.

The woman with the gold mask laughed. "Don't be scared," she told me. "This is a big honor! You're the reason we're all here."

I didn't understand, and my fear only mounted as Traynor pushed me forward onto the mattress. Stained in places, torn or threadbare in others, it had the sweet-and-sour odor of dried piss. While Traynor planted his hand against the scruff of my neck, pinning me in place, the woman in the gold mask cackled again, grabbing my left wrist. Someone else clasped my right, then one by one, they lay their hands on me, holding me down. I couldn't move except to turn my head, looking back over my shoulder as more and more people gathered around, an impenetrable wall of black masks watching me, crammed together, shoulder to shoulder, filling the room.

"Anathema," I heard a man say, then felt his fingertips slide up the back of my thigh. I tried to flinch, but couldn't. Someone else began to stroke the small of my back, another my shoulder blade, another my waist. Soon the crowd pressed in all around me, touching me, poking, prodding, caressing, pinching.

From the corner of my gaze, I saw the man in the red mask, Robert, approach. He'd disappeared among the throng, but emerged now, carrying something in his hand: a long knife, the blade winking with reflected firelight.

"Stop," I whimpered.

The crowd began to chant, a chorus that started off little

more than a hush, growing louder with each recitation: "Anathema...anathema..."

"Please," I begged, as Robert brought the knife toward me. I could see the pommel sticking out from his fist, something weird and ornate, like a bird's head. "Please don't!"

The crowd sounded like thunder now, the words bellowing from their collective mouths, shuddering through the air, drowning out my pleas.

"...anathema...anathema..."

please don't please don't oh god please

Clasping the hilt between his hands, Robert raised the knife above his head.

Please don't hurt me!

"...anathema..."

Robert swung the knife down. At first, I felt nothing, a merciful reprieve that lasted less than one-tenth of a second. Then, the blade sank deep and pain set in, searing, agonizing. I screamed, tears streaming down my cheeks, and bucked against the hands holding me, twisting my arms and legs desperately. He cut into my back, dragging the sharp edge of the knife through my flesh. I felt blood pouring from the deep gouges. All around me, the crowd began to cheer, excited and eager applause.

"Anathema!" they cried together. "Anathema!"

I JERKED AWAKE SO VIOLENTLY, I pitched sideways off the bed and crash-landed on my ass. Wide-eyed, sweat-drenched, gasping for breath, I whipped my head back and forth, staring all around in bewildered panic, unsure of where —or *when*—the fuck I was.

"Jesus."

I remembered the lodge, the burial site, Rodriguez. Shuddering, I shoved my hair back from my face, then clutched at the side of the bed as I stumbled to my feet.

Then I remembered the dream. And I *felt* it—a terrible phantom pain still haunting my lower back. I rushed to the bathroom, snapping on the overhead lights. I hadn't realized that dusk had fallen outside, the room growing shadow-draped and dim, until that blinding glare left me sucking in a sharp breath, squinting.

As soon as my eyes adjusted, I jerked my shirt off. I turned, craning my gaze, trying to look at my reflection in the vanity mirror. Then I undid my fly, pushing my jeans down. Pivoting once more, I stared at my reflection.

Above the cleft of my ass, I saw it, jagged slashes of faint red scar tissue I'd never noticed before. I couldn't tell what the lines depicted, if anything, but I got a good enough look to make my heart seize and leave me gulping for breath.

It wasn't a dream? Not a fucking dream at all, but a memory? Did that really happen? That son of a bitch—did he carve that into me?

I heard the door to the room open, the rustle and stomp of Rodriguez's footsteps. I ran out of the bathroom, wide-eyed and stricken.

"Josh—?" he began, then drew back in surprise as I rushed at him.

"He cut me," I gasped, grabbing the front of his windbreaker. "That...that motherfucker...I saw it in my dream. O-only it wasn't a dream, it couldn't have been, because there's something there. On my back...he...he carved something onto my back...!"

"Hey," Rodriguez said, catching me by the arms. "Josh, slow down. What's going on?" His eyes widened as he noticed I was half-dressed. "Why are you—?"

"My back." I pulled him toward the bathroom. "Look at my back. He carved something into me."

"Traynor?"

"No, it was someone else, a man he brought me to," I said, turning around. "Do you see it? That mark."

Rodriguez looked down but didn't say anything.

"Do you see it?" I demanded, my voice shrill.

"I see *something*," he told me. "Some red marks, maybe scars?"

"I had a dream just now, only I think it was a memory. I remember being inside that fucking house, a man cutting me."

"What house? You mean the one on the other side of the lake that's all boarded up?"

I nodded, turning to face him again. "Traynor took me there. It was full of people. They were all dressed up, and they had these...things on their faces." I flapped my hand demonstratively at my head. "Like bird masks with beaks or something. I don't know."

"Bird masks?" There was an uncertain edge to his voice.

"They were touching me. All over, all of them. And they were saying that word again, the one I heard Traynor mention after he took me: anathema. They held me down on a bed, then one of them cut me, a man in a red mask. They all started clapping. Those sick fucks...they were cheering him on..."

My voice broke and I forked my fingers through my hair. "Goddamn it," I whispered.

"Hey," Rodriguez said, drawing my gaze. "Let me see it again."

I couldn't tell if he was humoring me or not, but I nodded. "Can you..." I asked hesitantly. "Can you tell what it is?"

"Sort of. It looks like some kind of symbol. A line between two triangles."

"Take a picture of it. Please? So I can see."

He seemed reluctant, but reached into his pocket and pulled out his phone. Leaning down again, he snapped a quick photo of my back and showed it to me. I zoomed in on the mark:

"What's it mean?" I asked.

"I have no idea. Why don't you...uh, get yourself together, and come back out here? We can try to figure it out."

"Oh." I looked down at myself, realizing I was half naked. Tugging my pants up, I said, "Uh, sure. Give me a minute."

I closed the door, then pressed my forehead against it, feeling like a complete dumbass. What the hell was wrong with me? If he hadn't thought I was completely batshit before then, he definitely would now.

I buttoned my shirt as best I could, leaving the shirt tails untucked. I looked at my reflection, saw my hair sticking out, my eyes ringed with shadows, a day's worth of beard stubble on my chin because I'd forgotten to shave that morning. I looked like a fucking lunatic.

When I returned to the room, I found Rodriguez sitting in one of the chairs. He'd removed his jacket and shoes.

"Hey," he said.

"Hey. Sorry about that."

"Tell me what happened."

I sank into the chair across from him, then told him about the dream. I prefaced this by explaining how the Brennus mansion had looked vaguely familiar to me when I'd seen it earlier.

"I'm sorry I didn't tell you," I said. "I thought maybe it was my imagination. Then I had that dream..."

I'd showed him the book from the gift shop, and he flipped through it. "You said everyone in the dream was dressed up, right? Like for a party?" When I nodded, he leaned forward, showing me a page, the picture from the Summer Gala at the Brennus mansion. "Like this?"

I frowned. "I'm not making it up."

"I don't think you are. But I think your mind was still in a suggestive state after our session earlier, and when you fell asleep, your subconscious pulled images from this book and our discussions about Traynor today, then tried to tie them together with that mark on your back. It's probably something you never even thought much about—"

"I never noticed it before," I snapped. "Not until today, right before you walked in. I'm not making shit up, Rodriguez, and I'm not out of my head, either. Something happened to me. And it happened inside that house."

He averted his gaze, his expression doubtful.

"Let's go over there right now," I said. "Bust off the padlock and go inside. I'll prove it to you. I'll show you the staircase I saw in my dream, a big spiral one, and the room where they took me. The walls were blue, the paint all busted up and chipping. I'll prove it."

"There's no point in going back now," he said. "It's going to be dark soon, and there's no electricity connected. Plus, we'd need the owner's permission, or a warrant to—"

"What about probable cause?" I'd seen enough cop shows on TV to know that much at least. "You don't need anyone's say-so, or a warrant, either, if you have probable cause that a crime was committed. And I'm telling you there was."

He rolled his eyes, not in an exasperated way, more in surrender. He knew I had him on that finer point.

"We can go tomorrow," I said. "When it's daylight again,

we can check it out. And that way, you don't have to drive all the way back tonight. We can just wait and go tomorrow. Didn't your partner say you guys had a bunch of rooms like this paid for?"

"The task force does, yeah," Rodriguez said. "Though Ellis isn't my partner."

"Can't we just stay here and go back to the house tomorrow? Please, Rodriguez. Please. I swear it's not all in my head."

He looked at me for a long moment. "You know how much shit I'm going to catch from Ellis if I bring you anywhere near that scene again?"

"She doesn't have to know. All we have to do is get in. If I show you the blue room, you'll know I'm not lying."

"I don't think you're lying."

"You said you think I've mixed things up in my head. Give me the chance to show you I haven't. Come on." My voice cracked, idiotically on the verge of tears. "No one's ever listened to me before. Not really. They all said because of the drugs Traynor gave me, I couldn't keep things straight, didn't remember right. No one's ever believed me except Bree...and now you."

He didn't say anything, but I could feel the weight of his stare.

"I don't really have any friends," I mumbled. "I guess you know that already, huh? I don't...like getting close to people. I don't trust them. There's Paul, but he doesn't know...not about what happened to me. There isn't anybody else...except for you, Rodriguez."

I tangled my fingers together anxiously as I spoke, unable to lift my gaze to meet his. The longer he remained silent, the more I felt like a fool.

"You know, you can call me John."

I looked up and found him smiling at me.

"I kind of like Rodriguez better," I said, and he laughed.

Chapter 12

"I thought you'd have hit the road by now," Ellis remarked, approaching the table in the lodge dining room where Rodriguez and I sat eating dinner.

"We're going to hang out here tonight," Rodriguez said. "I don't like driving in the dark."

"What are you, an old man or something?" she asked with a laugh, though there was a hint of skepticism in her gaze.

"You're not heading back, either?" he asked.

"No. I'll probably stay through the weekend."

He waved his fork, indicating the empty seat at our table. "Want to join us, then?"

I didn't miss the disapproving glower she aimed in my direction. "What the hell," she said, pulling the chair back and sitting down. "They have anything good?"

"The catfish isn't bad," Rodriguez said.

"Do they have anything that isn't breaded and deep-fried?" The server approached, and Ellis ordered a Cobb salad and Diet Coke. Stirring the ice cubes in her water glass, she watched with bored interest as Rodriguez and I continued eating.

The two of them made small talk while she seemed to make an active effort to ignore me. Not that I gave a shit. I didn't like her any more than she apparently did me, but for the life of me, I couldn't figure out what her problem was. I also couldn't work out the dynamic between her and Rodriguez. He'd told me they weren't partners, but despite her being at least ten years older than him, if not more, she seemed comfortably familiar, enough to do things like snag a bite of food from his plate, or joke with him.

Maybe they're fucking, I thought, because, hell, I wasn't blind or stupid. Rodriguez was a good-looking guy. I could definitely see the appeal.

"Excuse me for a sec."

The server had just brought Ellis her food when Rodriguez dropped his napkin onto his empty plate and scooted his chair back.

"I'll be right back," he said.

He left, leaving an uncomfortable tension. Ellis began cutting up the boiled eggs in her salad into more manageable bites. When she noticed my attention, I wrenched my gaze away, pretending to be occupied with a point in space on the opposite end of the room. Other than the two of us, the dining room was relatively empty, and the silence felt oppressive.

"Tell me something, Josh," she remarked at last. Then, with a coquettish laugh, she added, "You don't mind if I call you Josh, do you? 'Mr. Finley' makes it sound like you're a middle-school math teacher or something."

I wasn't sure which I disliked more, her previous brusque incarnation, or this one. "No, that's fine."

"Did you know that Michael Traynor was only charged and convicted of kidnapping you? No charges were ever filed for sexual assault."

"I didn't get a say in the matter. It was the prosecutor's call."

"Because of the amnesia," she said with a nod. "But even if you couldn't testify about it because you didn't remember, there still should have been enough physical evidence to prove it had taken place. Scarring, contusions, that sort of thing. Curiously, though, when I went through your medical records, the physical exams you underwent when you were found, I didn't see mention of any."

What? I thought, struggling to maintain my stoic expression.

"Then I started looking through the statements you and Traynor gave police," Ellis continued. "You never alleged any sexual activity took place. And Traynor never admitted to any. The only thing he confessed was that he'd taken you against your will. He's never disclosed what occurred between the two of you behind closed doors, not even to his own attorneys."

"Meaning what?" I asked, bristling. "You need someone to spell it out for you? Draw you a fucking picture? I know— maybe if I'd tried a little harder, fought back a little more, I would've been torn up more to your satisfaction, then you'd believe me."

My voice had grown sharper, loud enough for the servers to glance over from the drink station.

Ellis smiled thinly. "I'm not calling you a liar..."

"Yeah, you pretty much are," I snapped. "Because unless you think Traynor and I hung out for nineteen days watching movies and shooting the shit, I think it should be goddamn obvious what happened." I shoved my chair back and stood. "You've been jerking me around all day. What the hell's your problem? Or are you just pissed because you didn't get Rodriguez all to yourself for a change?"

Her eyes flew wide and she cackled. "You think...me and Rodriguez? Oh, honey." She laughed again, then shook her head. "I'm not his type. I don't have the right kind of plumbing, if you know what I mean."

This time I couldn't hide my surprise, and she laughed again.

"And I don't have a problem," she continued. "I just think it's strange, that's all. The bodies we've found, everything that's come to light, all of it after Traynor said he wouldn't talk to anyone in prison except for you. It's quite the coincidence, if you ask me."

I pushed my chair back under the table. "Fuck this. I'm out of here."

She pretended to pout. "Boo hoo. And things were just getting interesting, too."

"I WAS THINKING about the bird masks you mentioned earlier," Rodriguez said. He'd met me back in the room about twenty minutes after I left Ellis. If she'd said anything to him about why I'd gone, or if he suspected some kind of confrontation between us, he didn't mention it.

To be honest, I was only half listening as he spoke. My mind kept turning back to what Ellis had told me about my medical records. She had to be full of shit. After I'd been found, I spent hours at the hospital undergoing a grueling physical exam, where they'd poked and prodded me, drawing blood, taking swabs, scraping under my fingernails, photographing every cut and bruise they could find. They'd made me stand naked on a large square of paper so that any forensic evidence that might fall off my body could be collected. I'd been cold, embarrassed, still in a daze, and, frankly, terrified.

It couldn't have all been for nothing. Going through all that, feeling like a specimen trapped under a microscope or a freak at a circus sideshow. They had to have found something.

"Is this what you saw?" Rodriguez asked, startling me to attention as he held out his phone. The screen showed an image that instantly sent a shudder through me: the same black leather mask with goggle-like eyes and weird, elongated nose that I'd seen Traynor wearing in my dream.

"It's called a plague mask," Rodriguez said. "Doctors used to wear them in the Middle Ages to treat patients who had bubonic plague. They used to stuff the beak part with dried flowers to cover up the smell from the disease."

He sat next to me on the bed. "It's also the same kind of mask you had on when the police found you," he said, and his voice had grown softer. "Do you remember?"

"I...I don't know..."

But that was a lie; I did know. I remembered. Somewhere in my mind, through the drug-induced haze I'd been in that night, I remembered.

That kid looked like something out of a fucking horror movie, the guy on TV had said of me. *Buck-ass naked, nothing but skin and bones. And that goddamn mask covering his head...*

"Josh," Rodriguez said gently. "Dreams can often be amalgamations of images and memories. Things that happened to us a long time ago, mixed with things we experience in the present."

He still thought it was all in my head, the dream I'd had of being with Traynor at the Brennus mansion. Like a one-two punch to my gut, another realization dawned on me: if Ellis had seen my medical records, if she wasn't lying about what was in them just to jerk me around, then chances were good Rodriguez had, too.

"You don't believe me," I said, meaning more than just about the dream.

"It's not that. I told you earlier. Your mind was in a highly suggestible state, and you'd just accessed memories that had been previously locked away from your conscious awareness. It's possible more came to light than we realized, and in your dream, your mind got things mixed up, tried to make sense of..."

He kept talking, but the words ran together like rain-splattered ink on a sheet of paper, growing indistinct. All I could think was that he didn't believe me, just like everybody else, not the goddamn prosecutors, not the court-appointed shrink, the reporters, or the doctors and nurses at the hospital who had swabbed, scraped, and photographed me. Not even my parents.

Did you read my medical records, too? I wanted to ask Rodriguez, feeling humiliated and ashamed, as though I'd been the one who did something wrong instead of Traynor. *Why didn't you tell me what they said?*

Rodriguez had been talking, but his voice trailed off as I stood without warning.

"Josh?" He sounded worried.

"Excuse me," I mumbled, brushing past him toward the bathroom. I locked the door behind me, then stood in front of the vanity mirror, studying my reflection. Not for the first time, I found myself hating the man looking back at me, the Josh who returned after Traynor, the one who felt like a stranger in his own life.

Stripping off my clothes, I stood in the shower, letting hot water rain down. It bubbled and swirled in fast-moving currents around my feet. Steam wafted around me, filling the shower stall, then spilling out in slow tendrils, creeping across the ceiling.

Tomorrow, I thought. *Rodriguez will believe me tomorrow when I show him that blue room. He'll know I'm not lying or imagining things. He'll believe me after that. He has to.*

Why the hell it was so important for Rodriguez to believe me—and why it hurt so much to think that he didn't—puzzled and aggravated me. I'd never given much of a shit about things like that. Then again, I hadn't given a shit about anything in a very long time, or anyone either, except for Bree.

By the time I finished in the shower, the entire bathroom lay shrouded in steam. Condensation had clouded the mirror, and after wrapping a towel around my waist, I stepped up to the counter to wipe it off. Just as I slid my hand across the damp glass, I caught a glimpse of my reflection again, only this time, something loomed behind me: dark and misshapen, the vague outline of broad shoulders and a head with what appeared to be twin pinpoints of fiery red glow, almost like eyes. With a startled cry, I whirled around, my feet scuttling against the cool, wet tile floor.

I caught the edge of the sink, saving myself from a fall. Between me and the open shower stall, a wall of gossamer humidity hung in the air, but nothing else. Hesitant, bewildered, I reached out, hand shaking, fingers outstretched, and groped through the steam, just to be sure.

Nothing was there.

All at once, Rodriguez's suggestion about my mind being in a messed-up state—or however he'd put it—didn't seem like a bunch of psychotherapy bullshit, and I wondered if maybe he had a point after all.

I DIDN'T GET much sleep again that night. The bed at the lodge, which had seemed so comfortable and inviting hours earlier, now felt too hard, the pillows too soft. The blankets were thin, and it felt weird not having Lucy stretched out at my side. Earlier, I'd texted to ask Paul if he could pick her up on his way home from the bar, let her hang out at his place until I could get back in town, and he agreed. Still, even knowing she was in good hands didn't make me miss her any less.

It felt like I lay awake in the darkness for hours, listening to the soft sound of Rodriguez breathing from the neighboring bed, the creak of his mattress whenever he'd shift his weight or move. I kept my back to him the entire night, so I'm not sure if he had better luck resting than I did. All I know is by the time I closed my eyes, it only felt like it lasted a minute before the alarm on Rodriguez's phone went off, startling me back to consciousness.

He groaned, and the alarm fell silent. I'd heard the mattress squeak, the blankets rustle as he'd rolled to shut it off. After a moment, the box springs grumbled again as he sat up, and he heaved a long, tired sigh. Next: shuffling footsteps against the carpeted floor, then the bathroom door closing. Only then did I glance behind me, making sure the adjacent bed was empty before I got up myself.

The two of us rode in relative silence from the lodge back toward the mansion. Rodriguez looked as rough as I felt, so I guessed we had both fared about the same overnight in terms of sleep quality. He'd grabbed a couple of coffees before we left, but the rutted roads were so uneven it made taking more than the occasional scalding sip a virtual impossibility.

"You sleep okay?" he asked, his voice hoarse.

I shrugged. "Yeah. You?"

"Like a rock," he remarked, which I could tell was complete bullshit just by looking at him.

That awkward tension between us remained for the better part of fifteen minutes as we bounced and jostled along. Finally, with a sigh, Rodriguez glanced at me.

"What did Ellis say last night?"

"Huh?" I said, playing dumb.

"When I left the table at dinner, and you two were alone. She said something that upset you, didn't she?"

I shrugged again, without comment this time, and he sucked in a sharp hiss through his teeth.

"Goddamn it. I told her to knock it off. Look, don't pay any attention to her, okay? She likes to play the bad cop, even when there's no need. Whatever she said to you, just ignore it."

I looked out the passenger-side window at the forest whipping by. "She said you're gay," I said finally.

A beat passed, then another, then a third.

"I get the impression she doesn't like me, so I asked her about it to her face. I figured it was because she had a thing for you or something, so I mentioned that, too. And she laughed, told me no. Said she had the wrong kind of plumbing."

Still Rodriguez said nothing.

"It's no big deal," I continued. "I mean, I don't give a shit or anything if you are. I just thought that was pretty fucked up, outing you like that."

He didn't try talking to me anymore along the way, which suited me just fine since I was still pissed at him. But when he pulled over in the middle of nowhere, I had to speak up.

"Why are we stopping?" I asked, for a second, worrying I'd gone too far and now he was going to lead me out into the woods somewhere and either beat the shit out of me, or make me hoof it the entire way home.

"Can't risk Ellis or the team noticing my truck parked up at the mansion," he said, killing the engine. "I thought we'd hike up to it from here."

He climbed out of the truck and walked to the back hatch. I followed and stood behind him, watching as he grabbed a small knapsack and a toolbox. From the latter, he pulled out a handheld bolt cutter, a heavy-duty flashlight, and several other items which he then tucked into the pack. When he finished, he slung it by the strap over one of his shoulders.

"You ready?" he asked.

All at once, I felt the same kind of anxiety that had gripped me outside of the prison on the morning I'd gone to see Traynor. My palms felt clammy, my chest tight, my throat even tighter. I swallowed hard, then nodded.

"Come on," he said, glancing down at his smart watch that had a built-in compass display. With a nod to indicate the right direction, he started off. "Let's go."

I followed him blindly among the trees, sticking close to him like I was a little kid or something, scared of getting lost in the woods. That wasn't too far from the truth, actually; if I'd fallen behind or lost track of him somehow, I would have been screwed. Even though my phone also had a compass app, I had no idea how to use it.

"You're pretty good at this," I told him. "Wandering around in the wilderness, I mean."

He laughed. "I was a Boy Scout back when I was a kid. I guess it stuck with me."

We waded through a light haze of fog that clung eerily just above the ground. Leaves and sticks crunched and snapped beneath our boots. The air felt cold, damp, and somehow gray. I'd remembered my gloves for the trip, and slipped them out of my pockets now, pulling them on, hunching my shoulders against the chill. The woods seemed unexpectedly quiet, with only an occasional bird call breaking the veil of silence.

Rodriguez drew to a stop, and I damn near face-planted into the back of his jacket. He stared at a particular tree where the faint outline of something had been carved into the trunk. Just above eye level, it was crudely hewn, no bigger in circumference than my hand. If I hadn't recognized it, I probably would have overlooked it altogether, never mind given it a second thought.

"That's..." I began.

The same mark that had been carved into my back, the vertical hatch mark flanked by a pair of triangles.

"Stop." Rodriguez held out his arm the way my mom used to when she'd hit the brakes in the car too fast. "Don't come any closer."

"What? Why not? That mark's the same as—"

"I think this is a crime scene," he said in a low voice, drawing mine abruptly short.

What? I looked around in alarm, backpedaling in reflexive horror.

"We found that mark carved into trees in the two places where we found the bodies."

"What?"

"The other area Ellis talked about yesterday, where the cadaver dogs hit, we found one cut into a trunk near there, too."

"The fuck? Why the hell didn't you say something before now?"

"It's an active investigation. I've already told you more than I should have about it."

"But..." I sputtered. "But that mark. You saw it on my back! I showed it to you yesterday!"

"And that's why I don't want you coming any closer," Rodriguez warned, looking at me over his shoulder with a grave severity I'd never seen before. "I can't take a chance on you leaving any kind of forensic evidence here by accident."

Contaminating the crime scene. That's what Ellis had called it yesterday, why she wouldn't let Rodriguez show me the other burial sites.

He pulled out his phone, snapped a photo of the tree, then began tapping on the screen. For a panicked moment, I thought he was texting Ellis, telling her what we'd found, but then he said, "I'm saving the GPS coordinates for this site. I'll come back out tomorrow, tell Ellis about it then."

"Do you really think someone is buried here?" I asked, looking around again.

"If there's a correlation between the other sites we've found and these marks, then, yeah."

"Jesus Christ," I whispered. How many children had Traynor killed?

"Come on." He checked his watch again, consulting his compass. "We'll go this way instead."

The woods felt even more ominous now. I studied every passing tree, checking each trunk for more of those marks. Finally, a break appeared ahead of us—the clearing where the mansion stood. Rodriguez stopped at the edge of the tree line, surveying the clearing. The crime scene van was already back, the forensic techs somewhere down toward the waterfront, hard at work. There was no sign of Ellis or her SUV.

Rodriguez glanced back, then nodded, leading me across the open span of overgrown grass and brambles toward the house. Instead of approaching the front porch, however, he went around the back. A sunroom stretching the entire breadth of the first floor had been built here, all its once-panoramic windows now covered with plywood and *No Trespassing* signs. The back door had been covered with not one, but two large padlocks fastening heavy latches in place.

"Keep a lookout," Rodriguez told me in a low voice, digging through the contents of his backpack. As he pulled out the bolt cutters, I could appreciate why he'd chosen this point of entry. We were out of immediate view of anyone driving onto the property, and likewise for anyone on foot, coming from the direction of the lake and excavation site.

With a grunt, he worked the jaw blades of the cutters into place on the first padlock, then snapped the shank. He did the same with the second, then handed me the bolt cutters. After working the busted locks off, he craned open the hasps, and took a step back as the large plywood panel blocking the threshold came away. The old wooden door behind it was locked, but it was old and rusted, and when Rodriguez gave it a shove, it popped open, swinging inward.

He stepped inside, glanced around, then motioned for me to follow. Once I had, he leaned back out and dragged the plywood paneling into place.

"You alright?" he asked, reaching into the bag again, pulling out the flashlight. I nodded, but the truth of my apprehension must have been obvious, because he smiled. "Hey, big deep breath. The hard part's over."

He led the way toward the front of the house. Although the barricaded windows kept the bright beam of his flashlight from escaping outside, they also kept the inside of the house as dark and shadow-draped as a tomb. Broken plaster crunched underfoot, and the narrow circumference of light swept over and around arched doorways, cornices, and friezes.

It was obvious that we weren't the first to trespass. Graffiti adorned the walls, and the floor was littered with empty beer cans, liquor bottles, spent cigarette butts, ragged old blankets, used condoms, and empty food containers. The air smelled stale, and as Rodriguez panned the flashlight, we could hear the hushed scuttle of tiny rodent feet.

Nothing looked familiar to me, not until we reached the foyer, and I stood, staring up the towering column of an elegantly sweeping staircase that wound its way to the top floor.

"What is it?" Rodriguez whispered.

"I've seen this before," I whispered back. "These stairs..."

I started up toward the second floor without waiting for him.

"Hey," Rodriguez said. "Hold up!"

He followed, catching up to me on the second-story landing moments later. When he shone the light around, I grabbed his wrist, freezing the beam as it illuminated a doorway to the left.

"There," I gasped, eyes wide with disbelief. I felt frightened again, my breath shortening, every muscle in my body tensing as if poised for flight or fight. Staring at that seemingly innocuous threshold, I could see the battered and chipped cerulean paint on the wall in the room beyond.

"That's the blue room."

When Rodriguez lowered the light, it flashed off something near our feet. With a frown, he picked it up: a gold sequin. I couldn't move, images of the woman in the gold plague mask flashing through my mind as she'd seized me by the face.

He's perfect, just like in the pictures! Don't you think so, darling?

Inside the blue room, the fireplace lay cold and dormant now. The mattress was gone, but the iron bedframe remained, headboard listing to one side, the footboard sagging toward the middle, all of it draped with cobwebs and rust. Nothing else remained except dirt and dust on the floor, small piles of windswept leaves and twigs blown in through broken windowpanes and down abandoned chimneys. A couple of empty bottles with faded whiskey labels, and a charred mark on the hearthstones, suggested someone had camped there at some point.

From the doorway, Rodriguez began taking pictures with his phone. Once he'd documented the entire room, he strode toward the bed, leaving footprints in the dust, as if walking through a snowfall.

My hand trailed unconsciously to the small of my back.

Anathema, I remembered the crowd shouting as the man in the red mask had cut me. *Anathema!*

It was real, I thought. *It wasn't in my head. It really happened.*

"This is the room you saw?" Rodriguez asked. I hadn't been able to step past the threshold, frozen in the doorway like a terrified child.

"Yes," I whispered. That strangling sense of anxiety I'd felt all along had swelled to overwhelming proportions now. My skin crawled beneath my clothes, as if ghostly hands touched me, tactile echoes of all the hands that had groped and fondled me in that same room years earlier. I wanted to go, to run back downstairs as fast as I could, out of that fucking house and back through the woods, back to Rodriguez's truck. The compulsion, the fear—the borderline panic—left me shaking all over, on the verge of hyperventilating.

Rodriguez continued taking photographs from inside the room, starting with the fireplace and moving clockwise toward the bed.

"So, can you dust for fingerprints or something?" I asked.

"We're not likely to find any after all this time. Plus, it looks like people have been in and out over the years. No telling how many have touched—"

From somewhere downstairs, we both heard a loud crash. It sounded like something heavy toppled, and I drew back with a cry as Rodriguez whirled around.

"What was that?" I gasped.

"I don't know. Maybe that piece of plywood over the backdoor just fell over." He glanced at me. "That's probably our cue to leave."

"You don't want to search the rest of the house?"

"Not especially. We've got what we came for. Besides, if the panel fell, someone's bound to notice. I don't want to get caught in here, do you?"

I imagined Ellis, her face somewhere between a scowl and triumphant smirk if she found us, quipping something like, "Well, now, Mr. Finley, funny meeting you here. And contaminating my crime scene, at that."

"Uh, not particularly," I told Rodriguez, who nodded.

"Good. Let's get the fuck out of here."

Chapter 13

By the time we hiked back to the SUV, I felt chilled to the bone. I warmed my hands against the dashboard vents while Rodriguez drove. He'd already texted Ellis to say he was driving me back home, so instead of returning to the lodge, he made his way back toward the highway. I waited until we reached paved roads again, instead of gravel or dirt, before saying much of anything.

"You...believe me now, right?" I asked him at last. "The blue room was there, just like I said. That's proof I'm not lying or imagining things."

"I've always believed you. I keep telling you that."

"Yeah, but..." My voice faltered, and I looked down at my hands.

He lifted his coffee cup out of the center console holder and took a drink. It must have been stone cold by now, and with a grimace, he set it back again.

"You mind if we stop in a bit?" he asked. "I'll need to get some gas at some point, and more coffee."

"Sure," I said, picking at a loose thread I'd discovered on the sleeve of my jacket.

I've always believed you. I keep telling you that.

"Hey, Rodriguez?" I said quietly. "Last night, Ellis...she said she saw my medical records. From after I escaped, I mean."

He made a quiet, rumbling sound in acknowledgement.

"Have you...seen them too?" I asked.

"Yes."

"She said..." I took a deep breath, feeling anxious and nauseous. "Ellis told me there was no physical evidence that Traynor did anything to me." Even though it made my abdominal muscles clench just to say it, I managed to spit out in elaboration: "Sexually."

Out of the corner of my gaze, I saw him tighten his grasp on the steering wheel. At the same time, he uttered a low, quiet sigh.

"I figured she pulled some shit like that," he said. "Like I said, she likes to play the bad cop. Even if there's no one around to be the good one."

"Is it true? All those tests they did on me, that's what they showed?"

Do you believe it? As hard as it had been to choke out the reference to sex moments earlier, these words felt even more impossible. I was too afraid of the answer I might receive.

"They didn't find any evidence of semen," Rodriguez said. "Or any bruising, lacerations, or other indications of recent trauma to your perineum. That doesn't exclude sexual assault, however. If Traynor used his fingers to violate you, or if he used lubrication, there could potentially be little, if any, damage. And if he used condoms, there'd be no semen."

He looked over at me. "In any case, sexual assault doesn't just mean penetration. Yesterday, when you went under, you described him lying next to you in bed, masturbating. That's sexual assault, too."

"It is?"

"You were a child. Whether he left evidence behind or not is irrelevant. The man's a sick piece of shit."

He believes me, I thought, finding myself ridiculously on the verge of tears. *He meant it. He's believed me the whole time.*

"I'm going to report Ellis for misconduct," Rodriguez continued. "She had no right to say anything to you about those records. Not in the way she did."

"But they only convicted Traynor for kidnapping. They never went after him on any other charges. It has to be because those exams—"

"Traynor agreed to plead guilty to all the kidnapping counts in exchange for the court dropping any sex-related charges." When Rodriguez turned, my shock must have been obvious. "You didn't know that? There may not have been much physical evidence, but the circumstantial stuff was quite damning. I mean, the police found you wandering around drugged up and naked, wearing a bondage mask."

"I didn't follow the trial," I said. "No one ever told me, and I've never read much about it. I...I didn't want to know..."

Like my father, I'd been determined to put that part of my life behind me, to pretend it never happened. I realized now that I sounded like a dumbass.

"Well, Ellis sure as hell knew," Rodriguez said, frowning. "Which is exactly why she was way out of line to say shit like that to you."

"I don't want to make trouble..."

"You're not."

"Between you and Ellis, I mean."

"You're not. Shit between us goes back a few years, when I first graduated from the academy. She's had a bone to pick with me ever since. You just got caught in the middle, and I'm sorry about that. It won't happen again. I won't let it."

Are you okay? Gordon asked me later that night. *You look really tired.*

Slapping on a happy face and jerking off for a virtual audience was the last thing I felt like doing by the time Rodriguez brought me home. But I'd put on a pot of coffee, chugged back a couple of cups, and hoped the caffeine would carry me through the show.

"I'm fine, Gordon," I told him, smiling dutifully for the camera. "Just a rough couple of nights in a row. Read into that what you will."

A smattering of responses populated in the chat dialogue, some laughing-face emojis, a few *LOL's* and *LMAO's*, and comments like *With who???* and *Lucky bastard!!* Nothing from Gordon, though, so to divert him from worrying, I switched tacks.

"Where are you tonight?" I asked him. "Still in Atlanta?"

In Annapolis now, he typed back in reply. *Staying through Friday. Ever been?*

"That's in Pennsylvania, right?" I knew it wasn't even before he corrected me. Annapolis was less than an hour from where I lived, but that wasn't anything I'd ever broadcast.

After the stream ended, I pulled on my jacket, then walked down the street to Lupin's. Even though I was exhausted, basically operating on autopilot and the last remnants of caffeine in my system, I wanted to get Lucy. Last night had been the first I'd spent away from her in I don't even know how long. Even when I crashed with Paul, I always brought her with me. I figured if I had any chance in hell of getting a decent night's sleep tonight, I needed Lucy with me.

"Hey, man," Paul remarked as I walked into the bar. "You just get back in town?"

"A few hours ago. Had to do my stream first."

"Like that?" he asked, brows raised. "You look like shit."

"Fuck you, too."

At the sound of my voice, Lucy came bounding from the back of the bar, her claws scrabbling on the linoleum. She charged headlong, then leaped into me, front paws first, right in the stomach.

"Hey, Lu," I told her, laughing as she lapped at my face. "Silly dog, yes, hello. I missed you, too."

She dropped back onto all fours, and I squatted beside her, letting the lick-fest continue as I gave her a hug. "Did she do okay for you?" I asked Paul.

"Are you kidding? She's been in heaven. Beth took her to the dog park earlier, and look, she painted her toenails."

"What?" I caught Lucy's front paws again, realizing her claws were now hot pink. "What the hell, man?"

He laughed. "Suck it, sunshine. My old lady loves your dog. You want a beer?"

I went to the bar, sliding onto one of the stools. "Yeah, whatever's on tap."

"How was your trip?"

"It was fine," I replied, watching as he poured the draught. "Just took longer than expected."

"You never told me what was up or where you went."

"It's no big thing. Went to this place called Horsehead Lake in Virginia."

"The state park?" he asked, surprising me. "I used to go camping there when I was a kid. What, did you go with your sister?"

"No, with Rodriguez," I said, realizing as soon as I let this slip, I'd made a mistake.

"The FBI guy? I thought you said he was looking into something that happened a while ago. Why's he still bothering you?"

"He's not. He had some more questions. That's all."

Paul finished drawing the beer and set it on a coaster in

front of me. "And he couldn't ask you here? You had to go all the way to Virginia?"

"Come on," I grumbled. "Let it go already."

"He ghosts on you for...what? At least two or three weeks, then out of the blue, wants you to go on a trip? I smell bullshit, man. I'm telling you, the guy's setting you up."

"He didn't ghost me. He went home for a funeral."

"Yeah, right."

"I'm serious. His dad had a heart attack in El Paso. That's where Rodriguez grew up. We met up when he got back in town and talked about it. He and his dad were really close. He's torn up."

Paul regarded me thoughtfully for a moment. "Sounds like you two are getting kind of cozy."

I scowled and took a drink of beer. "It's not like that."

"You sure, man? I've never known you to go out shooting the shit with anyone before. Except me, of course."

I shrugged. "He's a good guy, that's all."

"Pretty easy on the eyes, too," Paul remarked, and when my frown deepened, he laughed. "What? I'm just making an observation. And who knows? Maybe you stand a chance with him. Just because he has a wife or girlfriend at home doesn't mean he can't—"

"He doesn't have a wife. Or a girlfriend, either."

"Oh? I thought she called him the night you two came in."

"That was his partner," I said, realizing who the "Laurie" on Rodriguez's caller ID had been. "Another FBI agent he works with."

"Are they sleeping together?"

"Not likely."

"Why's that?" Paul asked, then raised his brows again. "You think he's gay or something?"

I scowled at him. "The fuck? Can you keep it down?"

"Who's here to listen?" He made a show of looking

around the bar, the few and far between chronic drunks languishing over half-empty whiskey tumblers and beer mugs. Then, leaning over the bar, he grinned. "So, is he?"

"I don't know. That's what she told me, the other agent. I asked him about it, but he never said anything one way or the other."

However, Rodriguez *had* said that Ellis had a bone to pick with him. His exact words. In retrospect, I couldn't help but wonder now if she'd insinuated he might be gay just to stir the shit pot that had been brewing between them.

"What are you going to do if he is?" Paul asked.

"What do you mean?"

"You like him, right?"

"I never said that." I frowned again. "I said he's a good guy. Quit reading into shit, will you? You're as bad as my sister."

Chapter 14

I was so drunk and exhausted by the time I left the bar, Lucy practically led me home. It was after three in the morning when I finally reached my apartment, and I crumpled facedown into bed, not bothering to strip off my jacket or shoes.

My bedroom melted away, replaced by dark oblivion, and I dreamed of Traynor, his breath in my ear, his body tacky, reeking with sweat, the nasty, humid heat of his skin, the crushing weight of him bearing down on top of me.

"Please," I tried to beg him. "Please stop…"

"Hush now," he murmured, only it wasn't Traynor's voice, but deeper, coarser, something so rough-hewn and ragged, it hardly sounded human. I recognized it, remembered it now: the man from the mansion in the red plague mask.

Robert.

I could feel him touching me, his hands leather-like and twisted, his fingers gnarled like an arthritic old man's, his nails elongated and sharp.

"Stop," I whimpered again. "Please, I…I just want to go home. Please—"

Robert grabbed my face, those talon-like fingers hooking beneath my chin, cupping my jaw, forcing my head back. When he whispered again into my ear, I smelled his breath, hot, thick, and rancid, like rotting meat.

"Anathema," he said. With a menacing chuckle that sent a shudder through me, he spoke again, words that burned themselves as indelibly into my mind as his knife had my flesh.

"You *are* home, boy," the man said. "You belong to me now. Forever."

SWEAT-SOAKED AND SHAKING, I jerked awake, scrambling up in bed and looking wildly around. My sudden movement startled Lucy, and she leaped up immediately, whining.

What the fuck was that? I thought, disoriented and panic-stricken. *A dream? A memory? Some kind of fucked up mix of the two?*

Gasping for air and on the verge of hyperventilating, I doubled over, struggling to fill my desperate lungs. Lucy leaned into me, trying to nuzzle the side of my face.

Tell me three things you can see.

Rodriguez's voice filled my mind.

Three things. Look around and tell me what you see.

I could see Lucy beside me, my fingers tangled in her fur. I saw the sheets in a rumpled disarray beneath me, and the fact I still had my coat on.

Breathe for me.

I saw my phone next to the bed, where it had fallen out of my jacket pocket. My hand shook as I picked it up, and I squinted as I tapped the home screen to life, the bright light sudden and blinding.

I meant to call Bree, because that's who I always turned to in the middle of the night when I had nightmares, but I must have hit the last number to have dialed me. When a man's voice answered, thick and groggy with sleep, it took me a baffled, bleary moment to realize what I'd done.

"Josh?" Rodriguez said. "What is it? Are you okay?"

"I..." I gasped. "I'm sorry. I didn't...mean..."

"Are you hurt?"

"N-no. It's nothing like that. It...it's just..." My voice broke, and I clapped my hand over my face.

"Where are you? Are you home?"

"Yes," I whispered.

"I'll be right there. I'm on my way."

I STUMBLED INTO THE BATHROOM, shaking two Ativan into the palm of my hand. I swallowed them dry, and chased them down with a mouthful of water I sucked straight from the tap. I then limped to the living room, crumpling onto the couch.

Lucy trailed behind me, hopping up to lay at my side in worried vigil. I touched her neck, working my fingers deep into her fur, wanting—no, needing—that physical connection to keep me grounded, my mind from drifting back to that dark, terrible dreamscape.

"Hey."

I'd left the door unlocked for Rodriguez, all the lights off except the lamp beside the sofa. At the sound of his voice, I opened my eyes, blinking dazedly at him.

"Hey," I said with a feeble smile.

He squatted in front of me. Lucy, satisfied Rodriguez was a welcome fixture in her home, didn't jump between us.

"What's going on?" he asked me gently.

"I had a dream. It...it was horrible. It felt so real." I'd let my eyes droop closed but opened them again. Feeling sheepish, I said, "I'm sorry. I shouldn't have—"

"Yes, you should have. And I'm glad you did. You can anytime."

For an instant, I forgot myself, the beer and benzos clouding my mind, and with a sidelong smile, I lapsed into Easy Mark mode. "I can what anytime?"

Rodriguez held my gaze. "Anything you want."

What are you going to do if he is? Paul had asked me. *You like him, right?*

Rodriguez lifted his hand and brushed my cheek. When I didn't flinch, he inclined his head, leaning closer.

"Josh..." he whispered, then his lips lighted across mine, settling gently. For a moment, he lingered like that, then I felt the warm, wet tip of his tongue brush across the seam of my mouth and press past. He lifted his other hand to cradle my face, then kissed me harder, more urgently. We fell back together across the couch, his hips landing flush against mine, and I could feel the hot, sudden swell of him through his jeans. I reached between us to cup his crotch, squeeze him there, and he drew back with a gasp. His eyes looked glossy, his face feverish and flushed, his hair tousled.

"Do you have anything?" I asked, meaning a condom. Even though I had a box of them tucked away somewhere in the apartment, I couldn't have begun to say where at that point. I was hardly cognizant of my own goddamn name, fixated solely on that moment, on Rodriguez.

"Yes." He nodded, his voice gravelly.

You like him, right? Paul had asked me.

Yes, I thought, because I felt safe with Rodriguez, more so than I'd felt at any time since my abduction. I felt safe with him; I trusted him.

I like him a lot.

I SLEPT MORE SOUNDLY that night than I had in ages, the kind of dreamless sleep that feels like you're floating in dark, fathomless water, no clue as to which way is up toward the surface, or down toward the ocean floor. It wasn't the alcohol, or the medicine that brought me to such peace, but rather, Rodriguez, the warmth of his body stretched out alongside mine, the weight of his arm across my waist, the comforting sensation of his fingers laced through mine.

My bedside clock read 5:30 when I heard the soft chime of the alarm on his phone, drawing me back to consciousness. He groaned behind me, then stirred, reaching past me to switch it off. As silence fell again, he leaned against my shoulder, nuzzling the side of my neck, his breath and mouth warm on my skin.

"I need to get going," he said, his voice hoarse from sleep.

I nodded. "Okay."

Despite his words, he made no effort to move, and instead pressed his forehead against my shoulder, reaching again to take me by the hand.

"I want to see you again," he murmured.

"You need me to turn on the light?"

When he chuckled, I felt his breath flutter against me. "I mean I want to see you again. Be with you like this."

"Why?" I asked, only half-teasing because this was too much, too good to be true.

"Because..." He kissed my ear through my hair. "I like this."

I rubbed the back of his knuckles with my thumb, whispering in admittance: "Me, too."

"I'll probably be in Virginia through the end of the week. Can I see you on Sunday?"

"I don't know. I think there's a Ravens game."

He snickered. "You said you hate football."

I rolled over so I could look up at him. Wrapping my arms around his neck, I tugged him down, and felt him laugh against my mouth.

"I have to go," he mumbled, his voice muffled as we kissed.

"So, go then," I mumbled back, making him laugh again.

Chapter 15

Without Rodriguez, I knew I couldn't replicate that incredible sleep, so I didn't even attempt it. I fed Lucy, ran on my treadmill for an hour, then took a shower and got dressed. This left me with nothing to do until midafternoon, when I was due to clock in at work. Sure, I could've cleaned the bathroom or vacuumed or some such shit, but instead, I went into the spare bedroom and logged into my computer.

Even though I didn't go to the District, I felt a momentary pang of guilt at the sight of all my livestream gear. Rodriguez said he wanted to see me again, and despite my better judgment, I wanted that, too, which meant at some point, an uncomfortable conversation would need to take place.

Would he be angry? Find it disgusting or sick—find *me* disgusting or sick?

These thoughts alone were enough to rile my anxiety up, so I distracted myself by doing something I hadn't done in forever, that I'd only ever had the nerve to do a handful of times in the last ten years.

I typed my name into the Google search bar and hit enter.

Rodriguez knew more about my time with Traynor than I did. He knew more details about the case and trial, and I was the *victim*. I'd lived through it. More than just ashamed of this realization, I felt angry about it too—with myself for never having found the courage to try and face my past.

The fact that Ellis also knew these details pissed me off even more. Before that bitch could throw something else in my face, catch me off guard again, I decided it was high time I figured shit out for myself.

Over 400,000 results for "Josh Finley" came up. Two hours and about five cups of coffee later, and I'd barely scratched the surface. I'd reviewed biographical information about me, the bare bones synopsis of my case, the trial. When I shifted my search from myself to Michael Traynor, I wound up tumbling down a whole new rabbit hole.

Jekyll and Hyde, the headline on one link read. It was a news webzine with an enlarged copy of Traynor's disheveled mugshot superimposed over a second, ghostly image of him, one in which he appeared in a business suit and tie, smiling confidently at the camera. The accompanying article read:

In December of last year, attorney Michael Traynor made partner at Mapother, Abernathy and Wynne, a renowned international law firm where, to that point, he'd worked in relative obscurity for the past five years. After spending much of his life in one of Baltimore's lower-middle-class neighborhoods, Traynor suddenly had realtors searching for a new home for him in some of the city's more affluent historic districts. He leased a new Mercedes and found himself on the invite list for some of the most influential politicians and lobbyists on Capitol Hill.

On the surface, fortune seemed to be smiling on him, and he appeared to be living his best life. However, when 13-year-old Josh Finley walked out of his house in the middle of the night, naked except for a ghoulish leather mask, the sick, sadistic truth of Traynor's hidden predilections at long last came to light.

The article went on to question why someone like Traynor, who had found financial and professional success after years of apparent struggle, would throw it all away. To that point, he'd had no criminal record, not as much as a speeding ticket in his past. Although police had discovered child pornography in his internet history and hard drive, on the surface at least, Traynor had seemed an unlikely predator.

I searched for the Corvus Society again, that stuffy group that owned the Brennus mansion. Something about the article on Traynor had struck me as vaguely familiar, and at last I realized why. Under the "History" link on the Corvus Society's site, it listed Allistair Brennus as the founding member, along with several of his friends: Stephen Adler, Arthur Livingston, Oscar Ludwig, and Henry Mapother.

Mapother. Same last name as one of the guys in the law practice where Traynor had worked. I looked up their website next, their "About Us" page. While there was no mention of Traynor, I found a biography there for someone else.

Matthew Anthony Mapother, LL.M, MBA, represents clients in commercial litigation with a focus on shareholder disputes and intellectual property matters, the bio page read. *His clients include multinational corporations, public companies, officers, directors, shareholders and...*

I studied the headshot of Mapother, struggling to find even the slightest hint of familiarity. There was none, and no mention in the biography of any affiliation with the Corvus Society. However, when I tried searching for the two together, I found another Mapother—Robert Mapother—listed as the current Chairman of the Board of Directors for the Corvus Society.

When I searched for both Matthew and Robert Mapother together, I found a few old stories from the *Washington Post's*

"Lifestyles" section, where the pair had attended philanthropic dinners or other charity events. A captioned picture of them identified them as brothers.

Matthew Anthony Mapother was a tall, elegantly handsome man with the kind of million-watt smile and chiseled good looks you see on politicians or movie stars. Blond-haired and blue-eyed, he looked like a modern-day, middle-aged Norse god. Next to him, Robert looked mundane and drab, with murine features and a long, thin face, his dark hair greased back. Despite obviously losing out to his brother in the looks department, Robert seemed to have had some luck with women. One image showed a beaming blonde hanging on his arm, identified in the cutline as his wife, Elizabeth.

I found more images of the pair at a variety of social events and fundraisers that had come and gone over the years. Curiously, philanthropy and public appearances seemed to be the only things Robert Mapother was good for. He wasn't an attorney, and it seemed he lived solely off his family's name and good fortune—the stereotypical trust-fund baby. That was probably what had attracted Elizabeth to him, I mused, as I found another image of her smiling radiantly at some fancy event, this time in the company of another woman.

Elizabeth Mapother and Audrina Gulbrandsen helped organize the annual Samhain Gala, one caption in the article read. *Each year, the Gala raises funds to support the ACoRN Children's Foundation, a Baltimore-based non-profit providing adoption services nationwide. Gulbrandsen is married to founder of web services conglomerate Datamaskin, and...*

Something about that sounded familiar to me, but at first, I couldn't place it. Then I remembered: my father had worked as a data analyst for Datamaskin years ago, back before my abduction. He'd left the company abruptly and, I always suspected, not on good terms, because it had taken him forever to find another job after that. Bree had told me once she thought maybe they'd blacklisted him.

From beside my keyboard on the desk, my phone rang, startling me.

"Hey," Bree said brightly when I answered. "You busy right now?"

Speak of the devil.

"Not really. What's up?"

"Want to grab some lunch? There's a new ramen place a few blocks from you. I'm dying to try it."

At least a dozen browser tabs were open on my computer, a potential labyrinth of hidden gems and dead ends. I hadn't learned much more about my abduction or Traynor's trial than I'd already gleaned from Rodriguez, and frankly, my head ached from useless information overload.

"Yeah," I said. "Sure. That sounds good. What's the address?"

THIRTY MINUTES LATER, I found her sitting at a table inside a restaurant called Shibuya Station, maneuvering fried dumplings from a plate to her mouth using chopsticks with a skill that, if hereditary, had skipped me altogether.

"Hey," she exclaimed, waving. "I went ahead and ordered gyoza. Hope you don't mind. I'm starving."

"Not at all," I replied, sliding into a chair across from her. "I'm running late. Couldn't find a parking place, so I had to park about a block over."

"You didn't have to drive. I could've picked you up. It was on my way."

"Last time I let you drive me anywhere, I wound up trapped at Mom and Dad's," I replied drily, making her laugh.

"You weren't trapped. They were happy to see you."

The server swung by to give me a glass of ice water, and I asked for a second teacup to share the quaint little pot of oolong Bree had ordered.

"How's work going?" I asked, reaching across the table to snag a dumpling.

"It's going," she replied, rolling her eyes. "We've got this big deadline coming up, and everyone's freaking out. And of course, today the client decides they want to change the font up to something a little less 'seriph-y'." She said this last with finger quotes. "So, I'm basically having to go through and update every block of text in a four-hundred-some-odd page catalog that's due to be uploaded to the printer's FTP in..."

I listened as she continued, nodding like I knew what the hell she was talking about. She worked in graphic design for an advertising agency, which meant she was usually griping about deadlines, impossible clients, lazy copywriters, or some such ilk.

"How about you?" she asked after the waiter had returned, delivering my teacup and taking our soup orders. "Anything new and exciting?"

"I don't know about that. I've been poking around on the internet some. Reading about the trial and stuff. Like how Traynor was only ever convicted of kidnapping and false imprisonment. He agreed to plead guilty if they dropped any sexual assault charges."

She nodded. "I remember Mom and Dad were pissed when they found out about that."

"You mean, you guys knew?"

"Yeah," she said, giving me a "duh" look. "They went to the court hearings. You and I went to stay with Grandma Ruth while it all was going on. Remember?"

My father grew up in Chester, Maryland, on Kent Island in Chesapeake Bay. At the time of my escape, his mother—who had passed away in the years since—still lived there. Prior to my abduction, my childhood memories brimmed with fun-filled summer visits to the train station, beach, and nature parks near Grandma Ruth's home.

"I thought we went because they wanted to get me away from the media for a while," I said, remembering how I'd sat on the side of my bed, watching my mother fold and pack clothes for me in a suitcase.

"It will be easier this way," I remember her saying. "You're never going to get back to normal with all those cameras flashing in your face all the time."

Traynor's trial had taken place ten months after my rescue, and more than six months after my failed attempt to return to school. My parents had struggled, uncertain what to do with me or how to handle me anymore. Despite what Mom told me at the time, I'd always had the impression they'd shipped me off to Grandma Ruth because they'd simply had enough of me and needed a break for a while.

"They didn't want you hearing about the trial every day," Bree said. "It was all over the news, and they didn't want it to upset you."

"I didn't know that."

"There's lots of stuff you don't know. Mom and Dad never talk about it. I guess they have their reasons, and you've never seemed big on the idea, either. Not until recently."

The server brought us our food, placing large bowls of steaming noodle soup in front of us. An awkward silence settled between us while Bree took a delicate sip of broth, blowing against it first through a slight purse in her lips.

"Why the change?" she asked. "You've always been so dead-set against finding out anything about what happened. Now, all of a sudden, it's all you can talk about."

"No, it's not."

"Is it that guy with the FBI? The one who set you up to meet with Traynor. Is he still bothering you?"

"His name's Rodriguez. And no, he's not bothering me. He asked for my help. They're investigating Traynor for other things now. I told you before."

"I thought he just wanted you to go that one time, ask Traynor about that kid."

"More has come up since then. He thinks I can still help."

She frowned. "More, like what?"

"Like the dead kid I saw when he first took me wasn't actually dead," I said. Bree's eyes widened. "He hypnotized me, and I remembered. I saw him, plain as—"

"Wait, what? Who hypnotized you?"

"Rodriguez. He's—"

"Have you lost your mind? You let him hypnotize you? He could've done anything to you, Josh, made you think anything he—"

"No, he wouldn't. That's not how hypnosis works."

"Oh, really?" She looked dubious. "And who told you that? Rodriguez? You don't even know him."

"Yeah, I do. I trust him. He's my friend."

She'd opened her mouth to argue further, but snapped it shut at this last. She knew as well as I did that I could count the number of people I considered friends on one hand and still have fingers to spare.

"Anyway," I said, plowing ahead before she could try to find out more. "I want to help him if I can. Especially if it means keeping Traynor locked away for good."

Bree still looked dubious, but said nothing. Using her chopsticks, she jabbed at the noodles and vegetables in her bowl, stirring them together.

"You said there's lots of stuff I don't know," I said, drawing her gaze. "With Mom and Dad, I mean. Like what?"

"Like they went to the trial every day while we stayed with Grandma Ruth. And they were devastated when the other charges against Traynor were dropped. There's plenty of stuff from before, too."

I cocked my head, puzzled.

"People did shit all the time when you were gone," Bree said. "They'd say they were psychics, or private investigators, always trying to get money out of Mom and Dad. Like one afternoon, a lady came up to Mom at the pick-up line at school. She knocked on the car window and when Mom rolled it down, the lady said she was a psychic, and she knew you were dead. You'd been drowned in the Potomac River, she said, and when I came out of school, I found Mom sitting there, behind the wheel, bawling her eyes out."

My stomach had tightened into an anxious knot, and suddenly, the ramen that had sounded so appealing when I ordered it looked and smelled anything but.

"Be careful, Josh," Bree said quietly. "I think it's great that you want to do this, that you feel ready now. But the world's full of people like that...who lie, who tell half-truths. Don't believe everything you see on the internet. Or think you remember under hypnosis."

That last one felt like a direct jab at Rodriguez—or me, for saying I trusted him—and I scowled.

"No shit, Sherlock," I said.

"Keep digging, Watson." Hoisting a tangle of noodles with her chopsticks, she paused before taking a bite. "And maybe you could try to be a little nicer to Mom and Dad from now on, given what I told you."

My frown deepened. "I'm nice to them."

"Sure, when you're not avoiding them like the plague."

"I avoid everyone like the plague," I said as she slurped down a messy mouthful of noodles.

After we finished lunch, I grabbed the check, despite her objections.

"Come on," she said, holding her hand out expectantly. "At least split it with me. I make twice as much as you do."

"It just so happens that I've recently come into a windfall of sorts," I told her, handing the ticket and my credit card to the server. When they walked away, I leaned toward Bree, adding quietly, "I found a new fan on my livestream."

"Ugh." She rolled her eyes yet again. "My brother, the porn star."

"It's not porn...exactly."

"It *is* porn exactly, by definition," she said, and from her billfold, she plucked a twenty-dollar bill. "Here. I refuse to accept your tainted money."

I helped her put her jacket back on, then we walked to her car in the parking lot behind the restaurant.

"Would you do me a favor?" she asked once we reached her car. "Don't say anything to Mom or Dad, okay? I think it's good for you, trying to remember, but...it'll just upset them. They've tried really hard all this time to keep you safe from it."

"I know."

"Thanks for meeting me today," she said, then I surprised the ever-living shit out of her by giving her a hug.

"Thanks for inviting me," I said, tucking the twenty spot she'd given me into her coat pocket.

She felt this, of course, and immediately realized, judging by the way her brows narrowed as I stepped away.

"You asshole," she said.

"I love you, too." I flipped her a wave, then tucked my hands in my pockets as I turned, walking toward the sidewalk back to my car.

Chapter 16

As I walked out of the warehouse the following morning after my shift ended, I saw snow flurries drifting down, the first of the season. And of course, I'd forgotten my fucking gloves again. Once in the car, I cranked up the defrost and sat with the engine idling, hands clasped together, breathing in ragged huffs that billowed, ghostlike, in midair.

My phone buzzed, the screen displaying Rodriguez's phone number, and a different kind of warmth spread through, the sort that makes you smile unconsciously.

It also occurred to me that I should add him to my contacts list.

"Hey, man," I said, unsure how to answer now after what had happened. With Paul, I'd always kept things casual and at arm's length, so the mornings after we had sex never felt uncomfortable or weird. Like putting on an old, familiar pair of sandals or blue jeans, we'd both lapsed into our customary roles as friends, but since Rodriguez and I didn't exactly have that kind of prior bond, I was in uncharted waters.

"Hey," he said. "You just getting off work?"

"Haven't even made it out of the parking lot. I'm waiting for the heater to kick in. It's cold as fuck here. Snowing, too."

He made a murmuring sound in response to this, then was quiet. "Listen, about that site in the woods..."

Again, his voice drifted into silence.

"Did you find something?" I asked.

"I couldn't get the cadaver dogs back out today, so I had field techs grid it off, start excavating this afternoon."

"How did you explain it to Ellis?"

"Made up some bullshit story about how I'd gone into the woods to take a piss and stumbled across the mark."

I laughed. "And she believed that?"

"Probably not, no," he said with a chuckle. Then, in a more somber tone: "We found a body."

My skin crawled at the realization that when Rodriguez and I had walked past that tree with the bizarre symbol carved into the trunk, we had been trampling a makeshift grave.

"So far, it's just the one, an adult. But we'll go down deeper tomorrow, see if there's anything else beneath it. This one was pretty fresh, so they're hoping to pull more forensic evidence directly from the scene."

"Fresh?"

"Maybe dead only a month. Maybe a little more, or less. It's hard to tell from a physical exam when they're buried in a shallow grave like that. It's been colder out, at least at night, but we've had rain in that area, too, and the ground's damp."

I had no idea how he could estimate the time of death just by looking at them—or how many bodies Rodriguez must have seen in his career to even hazard a guess.

"We're working on confirming the identity," he told me. "We might be able to based on the personal effects alone, or from photo confirmation of the corpse. We found his wallet with him, his driver's license. He's from Trenton, New Jersey.

We've got our field office there coordinating with local police to see if we can locate any family."

"How long does something like that take?" I asked.

"Hopefully not long. Like I said, we found his driver's license. His name is Miles Pennington. We're cross-referencing it with hotel records and airline passenger lists from..."

Rodriguez continued talking, but my mind had abruptly stopped processing his words. At the mention of the dead man's name, it was like someone had just pulled the emergency brake lever inside my brain, bringing me to a sudden, screeching mental halt.

You said you like to play games. Is this one of them?

That night at Lupin's, the guy at the bar, the one who'd dressed like a Steve Jobs knockoff and had followed me into the bathroom.

I like games, too.

Hadn't he told me his name was Miles? I tried to replay the scene from the restroom at Lupin's, when he'd walked in on me as I was trying to leave. The glint of the overhead lights off the wire frames of his glasses, the crook of his smile as he'd met my gaze.

We can play all night, if you want.

"Josh?"

Rodriguez said my name sharply enough to let me know he'd done so at least once prior to this, and I hadn't responded.

"W-what?" I stammered, snapping out of my reverie. "I'm sorry. I..."

"You okay?"

"Yeah." I managed a feeble laugh. "Fine. Just...freezing my ass off."

"Sorry, man. I should let you get home. I was just... thinking of you."

The admission should have stoked that warm, fuzzy feeling in the pit of my stomach again, coaxing a smile, but instead, I couldn't stop picturing that night in my mind, that guy from the bar.

Excuse me, are you Mark?

"Be careful driving home," Rodriguez said to me.

"I...I will." I hung up the line, my hands shaking again, but not from the cold this time.

It's not him, I told myself as I drove through the snow. It spattered against my windshield in fat, fluffy clumps before dissolving against the vent-warmed glass, melting into droplets of moisture the wipers then swept away. My headlights cutting through the flurries felt like something out of a science fiction movie, like *Star Wars,* where a ship flies at light speed through an untamed galaxy.

It's just a coincidence, I thought, words eerily similar to those I'd offered myself on the very night in question, when I'd tried to believe that he'd called me Mark by mistake, by nothing short of bad fucking luck.

It can't be the same guy. How the fuck could it be? Just because he said his name was Miles doesn't mean they're the same.

Only...hadn't it been a month or so ago that he'd come up to me in the bar?

Maybe a little more...or less. Now Rodriguez's voice replayed in my skull.

"Not him," I whispered, clutching the steering wheel like a drowning man would a life preserver. *Not him, not the same fucking guy. It can't be. There's no goddamn way.*

Even so, once I got home, I ducked into my studio and turned on my computer. I searched the information Rodriguez had mentioned: *Miles Pennington, Trenton, New Jersey.*

Immediately, I found links to social media accounts: Facebook, Instagram, LinkedIn. Several men featured under the "Photos" results, but one in particular stood out: mid to late forties, wire-frame glasses, an all-too-familiar smile.

"Jesus," I said, clicking on the image, following it to an Instagram page filled with dozens of pictures of this same man in different outfits, different locations, with different people in the shots with him.

Miles Pennington, the account name read, and beneath this, with bullet points: *Classic Capricorn, Head of Marketing at @JerseyShoreMedia,* and *Certified Devils Fan!* He had 1,732 posts, and 157 followers. I might have learned more about him had I scrolled down the page, but instead, I shoved my chair back and stumbled from the room, wheezing for breath, my chest collapsing inward like a rotten trap door giving way.

I staggered across the hall to the bathroom and jerked open the medicine cabinet, grabbing my Ativan. My heart felt like it was about to burst out of my chest like in those old *Alien* movies. If I didn't get my breathing under control fast, I would hyperventilate and pass out.

Lucy whined from the bathroom doorway as I slumped to the floor.

"It's alright," I gasped, holding out my hand. She nuzzled me, and I crumpled against her. "It's alright...I'm okay..."

Except I wasn't. At that moment, I was very much *not* okay, was the complete and polar opposite, in fact. None of this made any fucking sense. As impossible as it seemed that this guy had known I was Easy Mark, it was even more unfathomable that he'd then somehow wound up in a shallow grave four hours away in the backwoods of Virginia.

A grave I helped discover, I realized in dismay. *One that was marked with the exact same symbol that was carved onto my back.*

"What the fuck is going on?" I whispered into Lucy's fur. There were too many coincidences, too many threads all leading back to a single source, one undeniable, common element:

Me.

Chapter 17

I want you to hypnotize me again, I texted Rodriguez.

After catching my breath, calming myself somewhat, I'd managed to shuffle into my bedroom. Lucy padded along with me, climbing onto the bed as I lay down, facing the side of the mattress where, less than 24 hours earlier, Rodriguez had slept.

There was no way I could tell him what I'd come to suspect, not now anyway, not over the phone, but if I was the common thread, no matter how impossible it seemed, then there had to be a reason, something trapped inside my mind, buried in my subconscious, hidden in my memories. And if that was true, then there had to be a way to uncover it, just as the memory of Avery being alive had been.

My message showed as delivered, but he didn't immediately respond. It occurred to me that he might be asleep. Then, after a moment, he answered: *Are you okay?*

I'm fine, I typed back. *I just want you to...*

I paused, my thumb hesitating above the screen, then tapped again, deleting this last. Instead, I typed: *I need you to help me remember.*

The message hung between us, delivered but without response. Then my phone thrummed in my hand and Rodriguez's name—now programmed into my contacts—appeared on the caller ID.

"What brought this on?" he asked.

"Nothing. I've just been lying here thinking about things..."

"Then let's think about it some more."

I frowned. "I've had ten years. That's long enough."

"Yeah, but you haven't wanted to undergo hypnosis up until a few days ago. I don't want you to go too fast, Josh, or push yourself too hard too soon. I told you; you could end up traumatized."

"I'll have you with me. I'll be fine."

"Josh," he said in that same patient tone my old principal had used the day he'd met with me and my parents in his office, that condescending kind that irritated the shit out of me. "I appreciate the vote of confidence. But even so, I don't—"

"I want to help you," I snapped. "That's why you came to me in the first place, right? I don't get it. First you drag me into this, push me to let you hypnotize me. Now that I'm willing, you want to bail. What the fuck?"

"I'm not bailing. I just..." His voice dissolved in a sigh. "I think we need to slow things down."

I bristled. "You didn't think that last night."

The instant the words flew out of my mouth, I regretted them, wished like hell I could take them back somehow. But of course, it was too late.

"Josh." From the other end of the line, Rodriguez sighed again. "Come on, man. Let's take a time out, okay? We can talk more when I'm back in town."

"Fine," I grumbled. "Whatever."

"Good night," Rodriguez said. "Get some sleep."

"*SHIT!*"

Lucy startled as I threw my phone against the wall across the room. It bounced off my dresser with a report like gunfire, then hit the floor. With a whimper, she hopped down from the bed and trotted out of the bedroom, which made me feel like an even bigger piece of shit.

"Goddamn it," I groaned, clapping my hands over my eyes. "I'm sorry."

I could say it to my dog, but not to Rodriguez, and in my mind, I kicked myself in the ass over and over.

Stupid, I told myself. *Stupid, stupid, I'm so fucking STUPID. What the fuck is wrong with me?*

I could have called him back and stumbled my way through an apology, or maybe even texted, but I couldn't bring myself to. Knowing me, it would only make things worse.

"Lucy?" I called. If I couldn't smooth things over with Rodriguez, at least I could try with her. "Lu, come on back. I'm sorry."

From the direction of the living room, I heard her collar tags jangle as she climbed onto the couch, her way of telling me to fuck off for having frightened her.

"Alright. I probably deserve that."

I slept for a few hours, a restless sort from which I emerged still feeling drained. A shower and a few cups of coffee did little to remedy or pacify. I had too much on my mind, namely the quarrel I'd picked with Rodriguez and how I could fix things with him again.

I wanted to help him with his case. The only reason he was being so cautious now about hypnotizing me was because of his feelings for me, which basically meant I was making it harder for him, likely more than it needed to be. At first, I thought about finding another shrink, someone who'd be willing to put me under, tap into that hidden vault of my memories. That might have been the easiest route theoretically, but I knew there was no way I'd find anyone else I would trust enough.

Lucy finally forgave me, venturing into the kitchen as I made breakfast, lured by the telltale scrape of a spatula against the bottom of a skillet while I cooked scrambled eggs. When finished, I scooped half of what I'd fixed into Lucy's bowl. As she dug in, tail wagging, I leaned back against the sink and ate my share straight from the pan.

And it hit me, just like a blow upside my head.

Traynor.

All these memories, locked inside my mind, all from a period in my life in which I'd been Traynor's prisoner. I couldn't remember them, but he could. Although I couldn't be sure if he'd tell me anything or not, he'd been willing enough to disclose the location of the burial site to me.

Maybe, then, I thought. *Just maybe...*

The idea of seeing him again, even through a glass partition, was enough to make my stomach clench, the eggs I'd just eaten churning anxiously inside. But I had no other choice, not if I wanted to help Rodriguez, make it up to him somehow for what I'd said.

I looked up the prison phone number and placed a call. As the other line rang, the knot in my gut tightened.

"Uh, yeah, hey," I said when at last, someone answered. "How late are your visiting hours today?"

BEFORE HITTING THE HIGHWAY, heading west for the penitentiary, I drove back out to the derelict neighborhood where Avery Ormsby once lived. This time, instead of creeping past in my car, I parked across the street from the rundown house where he'd grown up. Summoning my courage, and imagining Rodriguez's voice telling me to breathe in as I counted to seven...

...now hold that breath as you count down from four... three...two...and exhale through your mouth as you count down from eight...seven...six...

...I pushed the car door open and stepped out into the street. The snow flurries from earlier had given way to a cold, persistent drizzle, and I hunched my shoulders, ducking my head as I darted across the street, my sneakers splashing in shallow puddles.

I saw no sign of the dog the rusted fence sign warned to beware of, so I eased open the gate. My breath frosted in front of my face as I made my way to the front door. The screen door screeched on old, weary hinges as I drew it open, then leaned past to rap against the front door. The glass windowpanes, hidden from the inside by dingy curtains, quivered as I knocked, and I stepped back, tucking my hands into my pockets as I waited.

From inside, I heard a dog bark, not the deep, visceral sort you'd expect with a "Beware of Dog" sign prominently placed out front, but rather, something high-pitched and yapping, the kind a scrawny, toy-sized terrier might offer. After a moment or two, I watched the curtains covering the window flutter briefly, then the door opened a bit, fettered in place by a security chain.

A woman peered at me through that narrow space, cradling the dog under her arm, a chihuahua, I could now see, as it continued yammering.

"Can I help you?" she asked.

"Uh, yes," I said, tongue-tied and intrusive. "Yes, ma'am, I'm looking for Mr. or Mrs. Ormsby, if they're home."

I hadn't had a close look at the woman who'd stepped

outside to smoke when I'd gone by before, but from what I remembered, this was one and the same. Her hair, reddish blonde except for the roots, which were coming in silver, hung lankly over her shoulders, and the lines around her eyes, the corners of her mouth creased deeply as she frowned, taking me in.

"There's nobody here by that name," she said.

"Oh." Feeling even more awkward now, I took a hedging step back. "I...I'm sorry. I must have the wrong..."

I started to turn when she said, "What's this about?"

"I...I wanted to talk to them about their son, Avery. He's been missing a long time, and I...I just wanted..."

The door swung shut in my face. From the other side of the wood, I heard a metallic rattle as she released the chain, then she pulled the door open once more, wide enough this time to step fully into view.

"You knew Avery?" she asked.

"N-no, ma'am. But I was taken once...years ago, by a man named Michael Traynor. I think he had something to do with Avery's disappearance, too."

The woman studied me through the screen, then reached down, pushing open the door. "I'm Rebecca Kahn," she told me. "Avery's my son. Come in."

On the inside, the little house looked cluttered, yet tidy. Rebecca walked ahead of me, the dog squirming under her arm. She dropped it into a room along a short, narrow corridor, then closed the door on it, motioning to me with her other hand.

"In there," she said, indicating a living room. "Sit down if you want."

"Yes, ma'am. Thank you."

"You want a Coke?"

"No, thank you."

She shrugged, then followed me into the living room. As I

sat rigidly on the couch, she slumped in a recliner across from me. On the coffee table between us, I saw a pack of menthol cigarettes and a green plastic lighter. She reached for both, and lit up a smoke, tipping her head back to exhale a sharp plume.

"Michael Traynor," she remarked. "There's a name I haven't heard in a while."

"Do you know him?"

"I used to. A long time ago." Studying me thoughtfully, she took another drag. "What's your name?"

"Josh," I said. Wiping my hand on the leg of my jeans, I extended it to her. "Josh Finley, ma'am. Nice to meet you."

She smirked. "Charmed, I'm sure," she said, accepting the handshake. Her skin felt like leather, dry and rough, the meat and bones of her fingers beneath sinewy yet strong.

"How did you know Traynor?" I said. "If you don't mind me asking...?"

"We went to school together. He grew up right around here, you know. About four blocks south. He was always a bit of an odd duck, keeping to himself a lot, his head full of stars."

Rising to her feet, she crossed the room to a curio cabinet. She rummaged briefly through the contents before pulling out a slim, leather-bound book. She blew dust from the cover and carried it to the coffee table: a high school yearbook.

"Here," she said, holding her cigarette in one hand, and turning back the cover with the other. She flipped through the pages until she found what she'd apparently been looking for, then spun it around to show me.

Among the rows of portrait headshots for the senior class, I saw Traynor, his hair in a side-swept bowl cut circa mid-1990s.

"He knew Avery's dad from back then, too." She pointed to another boy's picture, a gangly kid with curly hair and freckles: Daniel Ormsby. "We were never married. He lived with me for a while until I caught him screwing around with my sister. Sent his ass packing."

Leaning forward, she tapped the tip of her cigarette against the rim of a ceramic ashtray, knocking a short column of ash off.

"Danny had a gambling problem. Got himself in deep with some loan sharks. I think that's why he must've done what he did. That, and to get back at me for kicking him to the curb."

"What he did?"

She nodded, her mouth a thin, ragged line. "He sold Avery."

"Wh-what...? To Traynor?"

"No. Mike was just the middleman. Set the whole thing up, Danny said. Some rich guy in D.C. who liked to buy and sell kids was offering fifteen grand for a white boy Avery's age. Mike mentions this to Danny, knowing he's hard-up for cash. So, Danny took him up on it. Least that's what he said. He told me all about it, the son of a bitch. He wound up with cancer all in his colon. Killed him in less than a year, about two, three years ago. He called me from his deathbed, told me what he'd done."

"Did you go to the police?" I asked.

She snuffed out her cigarette, then reached immediately for the pack to light another. "No point in it. They never took it serious anyway when Avery went missing. He had a habit of running away sometimes. He never went far, not for very long, but that didn't matter, not to the cops. They wrote him off."

Her eyes grew misty as she looked away. "I remember you now," she told me. "You're that boy from the news. The one they found in the middle of the night." I nodded and her expression grew mournful. "What'd Mike do to you?"

"I don't remember."

She made a thoughtful sound. "Probably better that way. I

don't like to think about what might've become of Avery. He was a troubled kid, sure. Came by it honestly from his daddy. But he was still mine. You never give up hope on what's yours."

I'd come that day to tell her I'd seen Avery alive, but watching the tears well now in her eyes, glistening in the pale light drifting through the curtains, I couldn't find the words. After all, what I'd seen had been horrible, and I had no idea what had become of him after that. For all I know, in the end, Traynor *had* killed him, or sold him to some wealthy pervert, like he'd told Avery's dad.

"Traynor's in jail, thanks to you," Rebecca said. "That's good enough for me."

I sure as hell couldn't tell her that Traynor would likely be out of jail soon, again, thanks to me. Because of my amnesia, I couldn't say if he'd raped me, not with any certainty, and without that conviction on his record, he could be a free man all too soon.

"How old are you?" she asked as I was leaving. She remained in the doorway, speaking through the screen door as I stepped out onto the porch.

"Twenty-three."

She smiled. "You're the same age, then, you and Avery, I mean. He'd have turned twenty-four at the end of this month."

It sounded so final, the way she spoke of her son in the past tense. Again, I couldn't bring myself to tell her what I'd seen on the day Traynor had taken me. It felt too much like a lie.

"Take care, Josh," she told me. "Tell your mama she's raised herself a right decent young man."

"Yes, ma'am. I sure will."

Chapter 18

"You look tired," Traynor said as I picked up the handset. "You haven't been sleeping well."

He said this as a statement of fact, rather than an inquiry, and I scowled at him through the glass.

"Wonder why," I said.

The corner of his mouth twitched up. He hadn't shaved, and the coarse stubble of his beard drew into a dark slash where a dimple indented. "'O God, I could be bounded in a nutshell, and count myself a king of infinite space, were it not that I have bad dreams'."

My frown deepened. "Is that supposed to be poetry or something?"

"It's Shakespeare. From *Hamlet*. The title character is lamenting that he can't find happiness or satisfaction in the world because of his own relentless, selfish pursuits."

"Whatever. I didn't come here for English class."

Traynor cocked his head. "Why did you, then? I have to admit this is a wonderful, but completely unexpected, surprise." He looked pointedly around the empty room behind me. "Did that agent bring you again? What's his name, Rodriguez?"

"He's not here," I said, drawing his attention again, full, unabated, and piqued. "It's just me."

He smiled again. "Why?"

"I..." My throat felt dry all of a sudden, and I swallowed hard. "I need you to tell me what happened when I was with you."

He didn't say anything, watching me with a flat, impassive affect I couldn't read.

"You were right before," I said. "When I was here last time, and you asked about my amnesia. I can't remember much, but it's coming back to me in pieces. Like when you brought me to the Brennus mansion."

His lips pursed, a puzzled expression. "Brennus mansion?"

"The place you sent us to at Horsehead Lake. You drew me a fucking map. You said Avery Ormsby was buried there. Only it's not Avery's body, is it? I remember that, too."

My voice had grown louder, sharper as I spoke, as tension ratcheted up inside me, tightening through my shoulders and chest.

"Who's buried there?" I asked.

"I don't know."

"Like hell," I snapped. "You sent me there. You knew exactly where the grave was. You're the one who dug it."

"I know where the grave is. But I'm not the one who dug it. And I don't know the boy's name. I don't know any of their names."

It felt like he'd just dropped a nightcrawler, cold, slimy, and wriggling, down the back of my shirt.

"How many are there?" I asked.

"Five. There are five boys buried there altogether." Lifting his hands in my direction, a gesture of supplication, he added, "But I didn't kill any of them."

"Then who did? Who killed them—and the others buried with them?"

At this, he looked genuinely surprised.

"Others?"

"Someone's been burying fresh corpses on top of the skeletal remains," I said. "Reusing the graves. Who is it?"

"I don't..." His voice faltered and he reached up, rubbing at his chin, his bottom lip. "How many are there?"

"I don't know. I'm guessing five. You said five kids are buried up there, right?"

Even though Rodriguez's team hadn't found that many yet, at least now he'd know how many to look for.

"Yes," Traynor said. "Although since you're sitting here with me, I'm guessing that no, there aren't five more buried with them yet."

It felt like another nightcrawler just slithered down my spine, bigger than the last, like the size of a boa constrictor.

"What's that supposed to mean?" I asked quietly.

He chuckled. "You're not ready to remember any of this at all, are you, Josh? Not really."

"Yeah, I am," I snarled. "Tell me what happened, what the fuck you're talking about. I'm not leaving here until you do."

"HAVE you ever heard of the *Codex Arcanum?*" Traynor asked.

"What is that? More Shakespeare?"

"No," he said with a chuckle. "It's an ancient manuscript, a companion to the *Lemegeton,* known in our modern age as the Lesser Key of Solomon."

I hadn't heard of that one, either.

"Solomon was a great king of Israel," Traynor continued.

"The descendant of David. He's considered a great prophet in the Jewish, Christian, and Muslim religions."

"You're saying God told you to kill those kids?"

"Not me. And not God, no. In addition to being a prophet, Solomon is regarded by many to have been a powerful exorcist. He's said to have compiled a list of demons and their hierarchal order in the *Lemegeton*. The *Codex Arcanum* describes how to summon them."

This just kept getting more and more ridiculous.

"So, the devil made you do it?" I asked drolly.

"No. The great Earl of Hell, commander of thirty legions —the Night Demon, Raum. And he didn't make me do anything. I pledged myself willingly into his service."

I shook my head and laughed. "You know what? I could've stayed home if I wanted to be jerked off."

"Wait," he said, and there was a shrill urgency in his voice that stopped me from hanging up. "I'm not lying, Josh. You said you wanted to know everything. I need to start at the beginning to try and help you understand."

"Then start making sense," I snapped. "I don't want to hear any more bullshit. You sold Avery Ormsby to some rich fuck, and I'm willing to bet that's why you chose me, too, why you let them cut me up that night at the Brennus mansion. There's nothing demonic about that, Traynor. It's just sick and fucking evil. You can try to pawn it off on the Easter Bunny for all I fucking care. It doesn't change the truth."

I thought it would catch him off guard, mentioning Avery like that, and the fact I knew Traynor had sold him. However, if it surprised him, he didn't show it.

"I didn't choose you," he said. "I was given your name and address. I was told to collect you."

A shiver stole through me at this, raising the hairs along my forearms beneath my jacket sleeves. "By who?"

"Someone who knew your father."

The words hit me in the gut like brass knuckles. "My... dad?"

"Yes. I followed you for months before they told me to take you. They tracked your every move."

"What the fuck are you talking about?"

"I worked at Mapother, Abernathy and Wynne for seven years, put in long hours, the shit cases no one else wanted, all to try and prove myself. It never did any good. I may as well have been invisible. Then, out of nowhere, I get an email that says they'll make me a junior partner if I bring you to them."

"You..." I stared at him, leaden and numb. "You're crazy."

"It's the truth. I tried at first to give them Avery, but they turned me down cold. They wanted you, they said. Only you."

"You're fucking nuts. And I must be, too, if I thought I'd get a straight answer out of you."

"The ritual you remember is the night you were consecrated," he blurted as I stood. "The mark on your back—it's a winged figure, a sigil of Raum. You were marked in consecration. He appears to his initiates in the form of a crow. He only assumes the human visage of the chosen anathema—his sacrificial vessel."

"This was a mistake. I never should've come here." I slammed the receiver down, cutting short anything he might have offered further in protest. Through the glass, I glared at him, huffing for breath, hating him in that moment more than I'd ever hated anyone in my entire life. He stared at me, pleading, still holding his handset to his ear, and pressed his fingers to the glass, as if in implore.

"Fuck you." I flipped him off, shoving my fist against the window, middle finger held high, then stormed out of the visitation room.

I WAS STILL SHAKING as I went down the front steps of the prison. The veil of misty rain had lifted, at least temporarily, but the air still felt cool and damp, my breath coalescing before me. I went to unlock my car door, then heard the crunch of shoe soles on wet concrete behind me.

"Josh Finley?"

I caught a blur of movement out of my peripheral vision, someone darting alongside me. I felt them hook their arm about my waist, and a hand fell heavily against my mouth.

I cried out, muffled, as the palm mashed my lips into my teeth, and I saw a flash of light against something metallic: a syringe. The needle sank deep into the meat of my neck, and I mewled around the hand clapped over my mouth. Whatever they'd injected burned beneath the surface of my skin. I had a half-second to struggle, albeit futilely, before the world spun around me, like a Tilt-a-Whirl at an amusement park. My hands drooped to my sides, my mind fading into shadow as the silhouettes of three men surrounded me, and I plunged into absolute darkness.

Chapter 19

"*Hush you bye, don't you cry...
  Go to sleep, little baby.*"
A woman's voice, lilting and sweet, drifted through the darkness.
"*When you wake, you'll have sweet cake,
And all the pretty little horses...*"
I felt my mind emerging from sleep, like a diver returning to the surface after a deep-sea plunge, drawn by that haunting melody.
"*Way down yonder in the meadow,
Poor little lamb,
Ravens and flies pecking out its eyes.
Poor little baby crying...*"
As I slowly became aware of the sensation of light, I groaned, my eyelids fluttering open. Everything in my line of sight looked hazy, as if viewed through a pane of rain-soaked glass. I could make out the dim outline of a person nearby, or at least their head and shoulders as they leaned into view. I caught a hint of floral perfume, and a blur of movement as the

person reached for me, soft, cool fingertips brushing across my brow.

"Don't..." I mumbled, turning my face from the proffered caress.

The woman giggled softly. "Poor little lamb."

My vision began to clear, like a veil lifting. The woman became clear, with pale skin and honey-blonde hair that fell past her shoulders in buoyant waves. Her eyes were large, dark, and doe-like, her full lips pressed together in the faintest hint of a smile. She wore an ivory blouse with a plunging neckline deep enough to reveal the slight cleft between her breasts. She sat in a chair beside me, one leg drawn up, resting her heel on her seat, her foot bare beneath the cuff of her cream-colored slacks. Sunlight winked off a pair of gold bracelets around her wrist.

Something seemed familiar about her, but my brain felt soggy and full of mush, the way it did when I'd come to at Paul's apartment after a bender at Lupin's.

"Who...are you...?" I groaned.

"Awwww, you don't remember?" The woman affected a playful pout. "Then again, it's been a while. And look at you, all grown up."

Letting her foot slip from the chair, she leaned forward again. I felt her hand against my crotch.

"You've gotten so big," she remarked, laughing when I tried to push her away. My entire body felt heavy and unwieldy, swinging my hand up and around like hefting a cinderblock by a fishing line.

"Leave him alone, Elizabeth," a man said, his tone bored. When I turned my head to follow the sound, I felt a momentary swell of vertigo wash over me, making my line of sight grow murky again. I saw the vague silhouette of a man standing nearby but couldn't make out any of his features.

"You're no fun," the woman, Elizabeth, complained. "Let me play with him."

Her hand remained between my legs, and she moved it now, her grasp tightening as again, she began to sing:

"Hush you bye, don't you cry...
Go to sleep, little baby.
When you wake, you'll have sweet cake,
And all the pretty little horses..."

I DON'T KNOW how long I was out after that. I had a feeling of weightlessness, like a dried leaf caught in a gentle current, bobbing as it drifted along. The next time my mind felt coaxed from that state of blissful oblivion, it was again because of a voice. Not the woman's this time, but someone more familiar to me.

Rodriguez.

I heard him speaking and tried to open my eyes, looking for him, wanting to find him. My eyelids felt so heavy, though, I could only peel them back in narrow slits through which I saw nothing but pale, diffuse light.

"...brief update on our progress so far..." I could hear Rodriguez saying, and his voice was somehow both close at hand, yet distant at the same time.

I tried to call his name, reach for him, but my hands wouldn't move, my voice no more than a harsh croak.

"Of course, Detective," I heard another man say, his voice dimly familiar, but one I couldn't place. With a chuckle, he added, "Is 'Detective' right? I'm sorry, but I've never found myself in..."

"Just John is fine," Rodriguez said.

"John, then. Call me Robert. And your name again, please, miss?"

"Ellis," I heard her say, her voice crisp and cool. "Special Agent Ellis."

"Yes," the man said with another light laugh, and if he felt insulted by her brusque response, it didn't reflect in his voice. "A pleasure."

They continued talking, and I couldn't understand what was happening, or where I was. They sounded nearby, but still, their voices sounded hollow, reminding me of the old cans Bree had once strung together when we were both kids, making a rudimentary "telephone" out of them.

"Rodriguez...?" I groaned, willing my eyes to open, forcing myself to rouse. As my vision swam more into focus, I could see the smooth, whitewashed plaster of a tall ceiling. Ornate corbels stretched across me overhead. With a grimace, I lifted my head and looked around at an enormous bedroom like nothing I'd ever seen before, the sort you'd find in a luxury hotel or one of those videos where you're given a tour of a celebrity's mansion somewhere in the south of France.

Where am I? I wondered. I sure as hell couldn't think of anyone I knew who could afford a spread like that.

"We appreciate you taking the time to speak with us, sir," I heard Rodriguez say, and I looked around again, turning toward the sound. I was lying beneath heavy duvets on a huge bed, and on the wall opposite a flat-screen TV. It was huge, wider across than I could have stretched my arms apart, and on its surface, black-and-white images were playing. I saw what appeared to be a living room or study of some sort, and three figures standing inside. One was a woman, obviously Ellis, with Rodriguez beside her, both facing another man who had his back to the camera.

What is this? I thought.

"I appreciate all the work the FBI and state police have done investigating this," the other man, Robert, said. "The

Brennus estate is on the National Register of Historic Places and has such an esteemed place in the history of..."

Brennus.

Why was that name so familiar to me? I couldn't remember, couldn't think clearly.

"...sincerely hoped in my tenure, I could see it restored to even some semblance of its past glory. Now, though, considering what you've told me..."

The words and voices seemed to ebb and flow, fading in and out of my mind.

"...and vandalism can be repaired," Robert continued. "But what you're telling me you've found...there's no way we could ever keep the property tied to us in any fashion."

"Yes, the Corvus Society," Ellis remarked, and again, that name felt like something right on the tip of my tongue, something I should know but couldn't quite remember. "I confess, I'm not very familiar with what exactly your organization does. I mean, I've looked at your website and everything, but to be honest, it looks like the typical D.C. good old boys' club."

Robert chuckled at this. "I assure you, Agent Ellis, we're anything but. The Corvus Society is a fully integrated civic organization, with membership open to any race, religion, gender, or political affiliation. Our purpose is solely to benefit our communities. In fact, to that end, we're hosting our fundraising Samhain Gala here tomorrow night. I would love it if you could join us for the festivities—and Agent Rodriguez, of course—as my guests."

"Sow-win?" Ellis repeated.

"It's an ancient tradition to celebrate the harvest," Robert said. "Samhain is held at the end of every October, when it's said the veil between us and the spiritual world weakens, allowing us to interact."

"I'll have to check my schedule and get back to you," Ellis

said drolly. "I may already have another spirit world interaction thing going on. But speaking of membership in your society, we've found a possible connection between at least two of the more recent victims. Their personal internet histories include a website called the Red Light District that's owned by a member in good standing of the Corvus Society, I do believe...? Sigurd Gulbrandsen."

"Yes..." Robert said hesitantly. "Sig is on the current board of directors."

"Red Light District hosts live pornographic web streams," Ellis told him. "Were you aware, Mr. Mapother?"

He visibly bristled on screen. "Most assuredly not."

"Both known victims subscribed to Red Light District," she continued. "They frequented channels for several specific models there. We subpoenaed records for each of the victims' accounts to verify which models, if any, they had been in contact with prior to their deaths. Of those they subscribed to, they exchanged online messages with only one in common, who goes by the screen name of Easy Mark."

What? No, no, no...!

With a grimace, I shoved the blankets away from me. Just the simple act of swinging my legs around, sitting up on the side of the bed, left me reeling and spent, gasping for breath like an emphysemic old man.

"The model is a man?" Robert asked on the screen, sounding surprised.

"Yes." Ellis sat across from Robert, laying a leather messenger bag she'd carried over her shoulder onto a coffee table between them. From this, she withdrew several papers or folders; I couldn't discern which. Tapping one, she showed it to him. "This man."

No, I thought again, eyes widening. I wanted to say it out loud, scream it at the top of my lungs. *No, no, no, no!*

Robert lifted the sheet and regarded it in silence.

"His name is Josh Finley," Ellis said.

No!

"Both known victims exchanged messages with Mr. Finley through the Red Light District website in the days leading up to their disappearances," Ellis said. "They made arrangements to meet with him in person, and have sex with him for money."

What? I thought again, my dismay growing. "No..." I gasped, leaning heavily against the bed, forcing myself to get up. "That's...not true..."

I couldn't see Rodriguez's expression, but he stood rigidly in the camera's view, as if carved out of a ship's mast. Stumbling, my knees buckling, my legs clumsy and weak, I made my way from the bed toward the far wall. "Rodriguez," I pleaded, pressing my hands against the screen.

"...our prime suspect right now," Ellis was saying, and I shook my head.

"No," I said. "No, that isn't true. I...I never..."

"...and concern that he's connected to the Corvus Society somehow, specifically the Brennus estate, since he seems to have an uncanny familiarity with where the previous bodies had been buried. The only way he could do so would be through Michael Traynor, a man who abducted him when Mr. Finley was a child."

"Do you know him, Mr. Mapother?" Rodriguez asked. "He used to work for your brother's law firm. He was a partner, in fact, up until ten years ago."

"I'm afraid I know little about Matthew's business," Robert said with a light laugh. "It's one of the largest law firms in the United States, however. I doubt even Matthew can keep track of all his partners."

"Michael Traynor was convicted of kidnapping Josh Finley," Rodriguez said. "We believe he may have been responsible for the deaths of the children we've recovered from your estate. Traynor's been an inmate at the Hagerstown Correctional Institute for the past ten years. Well, at least up until a week ago, when he was found dead in his prison cell."

I stumbled backwards, away from the TV. "Wh-what...?"

On screen, Robert leaned back in his seat, as if absorbing this. "How disturbing."

A week ago? No, that can't be right.

The last thing I recalled with any clarity was sitting across from Traynor in the prison visitation area. He'd been spouting some bullshit about God or something like that.

No, not God. He was talking about...

"Traynor had a guest who came to see him on the day he died," Rodriguez said, stepping forward and pointing to the sheet of paper in Robert's hands. "Josh Finley."

"The model from that website? You mean, they were colluding somehow, burying their victims in the same places? To what end?"

"No," I whispered. "No, no, it wasn't me."

"We don't know," Ellis said. "And unfortunately, we can no longer ask either of them for more details, since Traynor is dead. As for Mr. Finley—"

"He's missing," Rodriguez cut in. "His car was found in the prison parking lot, but there's been no sign of him since he met with Traynor last week."

"But we believe he's alive," Ellis added. "In hiding, perhaps. We also believe Mr. Finley has other victims we haven't discovered yet, buried somewhere on the Brennus property."

You don't believe that, do you? I thought wildly, staring at Rodriguez on the screen. *Oh, God, you can't believe that. Please say you don't. You can't believe I'd ever...!*

I pressed the heel of my hand against my forehead, trying to steady the see-sawing view in front of me. My chest had seized with anxiety, smothering my breath. I dropped to my knees, panting for air.

It's not true, I thought. *Rodriguez, please, you have to help. You have to believe me. Nothing Ellis said is true!*

"We'd like to expand our search on the estate," Ellis said. "Bring cadaver dogs and additional forensics teams in to broaden our scope." With a thin smile, she added, "With your permission."

"Of course," Robert said. "Yes. Anything you need. I'm more than happy to oblige."

"As we said before, since you've cooperated so much in our investigation, as a courtesy to you and the Corvus Society, we'll do our best to keep a lid on this for as long as possible," Rodriguez said. "But given the scope so far, I'm afraid that at some point, word will get out."

"Of course," Robert said. "I understand. It can't be helped. I'm grateful for your discretion in the meantime. And for keeping me apprised of your progress."

No, I thought in dismay, as I watched Rodriguez shake hands with him on the screen. *No, don't go. Don't leave!*

"We'll be back in touch soon," Rodriguez said. If he was there in the building, I had to reach him somehow. Maybe if I shouted, he could hear me? But when I opened my mouth, tried to scream his name, little more than a rasping croak escaped.

"Rodriguez...!" My legs went out from under me, refusing to bear my weight any longer. With a crash, I toppled to the floor, banging the side of my head hard enough to rattle my teeth and leave me blinking dazedly against stars. "Don't... go..."

Chapter 20

"What I fail to understand, Mr. Finley..." Robert Mapother closed his fist in my hair, then wrenched my head back, yanking me into consciousness. "...is why you're doing any of this."

The warm, welcoming man speaking with Rodriguez and Ellis was gone. In his place was this version, all furrowed brows, glinting eyes, and teeth clenched in a snarl. I'd come to be sitting in a chair somehow, with my arms behind me. I tried to move them, to release some of the painful strain on my shoulders, but couldn't. I felt the sharp edge of plastic, like a zip tie, cutting into my wrists and realized I'd been bound.

"Tell me, you little fuck," Robert snapped, jerking my hair, sending searing pain through my scalp. "Is it money you want? Go talk to your father, then. God knows we offered him plenty."

"My...my father...?" What the fuck was he talking about? My mind felt soft and pliable inside, like saltwater taffy being pulled.

"It's still my time," Robert seethed, leaning so close, his spittle peppered my face. "I have seven years. Whatever you and that son of a bitch Traynor might have been playing at, you just wait your fucking turn."

For each of these last words, he gave my head an emphatic shake.

"I don't want your money," I gasped. "Please...I don't know what you're talking about. Just let me go!"

It felt like tumblers in a lock fell abruptly into place and I remembered the dream in which I'd begged Robert in nearly the same way, those exact words.

Please...I just want to go home...!

"It's you," I whispered, staring up at him in horrified realization. "The man in the red mask...the one who cut me...!"

For a split second, I must have caught him off guard, because his fingers slackened against my hair. Then his eyes glinted with fury, and he coiled his other hand into a fist, punching me in the cheek. He hit me hard enough to make the chair wobble sideways, tipping onto two legs before settling again. I tasted blood in my mouth, felt it start to trickle in a thin, hot stream from my nose toward my lip.

I heard a high-pitched cackle come from behind Robert somewhere: Elizabeth, the woman I'd seen when I first came to. I realized now where I'd met her before, too—that same night at the Brennus mansion, when she'd worn the gold plague mask.

"Bastard," Robert hissed at me. "All you had to do was stay hidden and live your life. We would've left you alone for another seven years."

"What...are you talking about...? You're crazy. Both of you...fucking nuts..."

Robert punched me again, then a third time for good measure, and as my mind swam out of focus, blood streaming from both nostrils now, running off my chin and into my lap, I heard Elizabeth laugh again.

"Now, darling," she said. "Stop hitting him in the face. I want to keep him pretty for a little while longer."

I DON'T KNOW how long I was out after that, but when I came back around, I remained tied to the chair, my arms behind me. I'd been in this position long enough for the muscles bridging my shoulders to feel knotted and aching. I tasted the metallic bitterness of old blood in my mouth and groaned.

"Hush now," Elizabeth murmured, on her knees in front of me. My foot rested between her breasts, and she cradled my heel with one hand, a nail polish brush in the other. I watched, dazed, as she swept it lightly across the tip of one of my toes, applying a coat of soft pink. Tilting her face down, she pursed her lips and huffed a soft breath to dry the polish.

"What...are you doing?" I croaked.

She looked up at me and smiled. "Making you pretty again."

She wore a rust-colored sleeveless gown with a neckline that plunged nearly to her navel, and a skirt that lay billowed around her like the petals of an unfurled dahlia. Her dark blonde hair had been gathered in a loose chignon against the nape of her neck, and sparkling jeweled earrings cascaded from her earlobes. She looked like she was on her way to a party of some sort, but showed no inclination to leave. Instead, she blew against my toes again, then lifted the brush once more, dabbing at the next toenail. As she did, she began to sing:

"Hush you bye, don't you cry...
Go to sleep, little baby.
When you wake, you'll have sweet cake,
And all the pretty little horses..."

"Why are you doing this?" I asked. "What do you want from me?"

"That," she told me, reaching down to dip the brush into the glass jar of polish, "depends on who you ask." Again, she glanced up at me, blowing softly across my foot. "Robert wants to keep you here, locked away like in a fairy tale for at least the next seven years."

"Wh-what? Why? What happens in seven years?"

The corners of her mouth hinted at a smile. "You'll get sweet cake, of course. And all the pretty little horses."

As she painted the next toenail, she began to hum, then sing:

"Way down yonder in the meadow,
Poor little lamb,
Ravens and flies pecking out its eyes.
Poor little baby crying..."

Her voice faded, and she set the brush aside again. "As for me, what I'd like is to fuck your brains out."

I stared at her for a moment. Then, with a dry bark of laughter, I said, "Sorry. You don't have the right plumbing."

Her eyes flew wide, her mouth even more so, and she threw back her head, cackling. Slapping my foot away from her chest, she rose to her feet and lunged at me, clasping my face between her hands. I grimaced as she dug her nails into my temples, her thumbs pushing beneath my eyes.

"Careful, little lamb," she purred. "Or I'll peck out your eyes."

"Come on, Elizabeth," I heard another woman say from the bedroom doorway, a willowy blonde in an icy blue dress, her arms folded across her chest.

"Robert told me to come get you," she said. "Everyone's waiting downstairs."

Elizabeth held her gaze riveted to mine, her lips poised in a brittle smile. She leaned in as if she meant to kiss me, and I stiffened, moving to jerk away. Instead, though, she licked me, drawing the blade of her tongue from my chin, over my mouth, up to the underside of my nose. As I shook my head, sputtering in revolted surprise, she stepped back from me, smirking.

"Coming, Audrina." With a flutter of her skirt, she whirled around and walked away, leaving me with half-painted toenails, tied to a chair.

How long have I been here?

Rodriguez said Traynor had died a week ago, but since I had no way of knowing how long ago that footage had been shot, I couldn't be sure that's how long I'd been missing. The TV screen had remained dark ever since then, and I couldn't help but feel it had been deliberate, showing me Rodriguez, making me listen to Ellis's crazy allegations.

How long had he known about the Red Light District—and Easy Mark? I hadn't been able to make out his face in the camera footage, but I'd seen the tension in his posture when Ellis had brought it up, and wished I could explain. I wished I'd told him about it all when I'd had the chance, because now it had to make Ellis's suspicions about me seem more credible. After all, if I'd lied to him about that, even if only by omission, it would be natural for him to think I might be capable of something worse.

But murder? Surely to Christ, Rodriguez wouldn't believe I could do something like that.

I'm being set up. Someone's doing this to me, trying to make me out to be a murderer.

I wished I could tell Rodriguez, but I knew it sounded like bullshit. After all, to pull it off, someone would not only have to know I was Easy Mark, but also my connection to Traynor, and the locations where all the children had been buried—not just the general area, but precise locations, so they could bury their victims in the same graves.

It wasn't me, Rodriguez, I thought, even though I had no other explanation, no proof of my innocence, no fucking clue who it might have really been. *Please believe me. I didn't do it. I could never...!*

I looked around for any sign of the clothes I'd been wearing on the day I'd visited Traynor in prison. I now wore an unfamiliar T-shirt and sweatpants, and my clothes, as well as my wallet and phone, were missing. I had to find them, or at least the phone. The only way I'd have any hope in hell of convincing Rodriguez of the truth was to reach him somehow.

My hands were bound behind me, but as I moved in the chair, I realized I hadn't been tied directly to it, which meant if I was careful, I could get up. This, however, proved easier said than done. They'd been drugging me, and my legs felt as wobbly and unstable as a newborn colt's. After a few clumsy attempts, I wound up pitching sideways, crashing to the floor, chair and all. A rug helped to muffle the noise, but I lay there, motionless, holding my breath, waiting to see if anyone would come to investigate. Nothing happened, however, and I managed to squirm and crawl away from the chair. Without the use of my hands, it was too hard to stand up from this position, so I crawled over to the side of the bed and leaned against it with my shoulder, bracing myself as I stumbled to my feet.

Inching backwards, I approached one of the bedside tables. I craned my head to look back over my shoulder, fumbling with the drawer latch until I was able to tug it open. My phone wasn't inside. It wasn't in any of the other drawers or cabinets I was able to get into, either.

Goddamn it. There was no sign of a landline extension anywhere, and when I tried my luck with the bedroom door handle, I found it locked from the opposite side. The room had several large windows along a far wall, but through them, I only saw a garden or courtyard below, dimly lit by lighting recessed along a cobblestone walking path. No other buildings nearby, and no cars or people passing to try and signal for help.

In other words, I was fucked.

I still couldn't figure out what Robert and Elizabeth wanted from me. Nothing they said made any sense, and trying to combine it somehow in my mind with what Rodriguez's investigation had turned up to date, not to mention what Traynor had told me in prison, just made me even more confused.

One thing I kept coming back to was something Robert had said to me: *Is it money you want? Go talk to your father, then. God knows we offered him plenty.*

Was Dad involved in this?

Something Avery Ormsby's mother had said nagged at me, like a tree branch scraping against a windowpane in the wind, a persistent aggravation.

Mike was just the middleman. Set the whole thing up, Danny said. Some rich guy in D.C. who liked to buy and sell kids was offering fifteen grand for a white boy Avery's age.

I remembered after Dad lost his position with Datamaskin, we'd been strapped for cash, with only his military pension to tide us over until he eventually found another job. We'd had to sell our house and move into a smaller one. Even after that, I'd heard him and Mom arguing over bills when they thought Bree and I had gone to bed for the night, how we'd even had to go without cable TV and internet service for a time because we hadn't been able to afford it.

Fifteen thousand dollars would've looked pretty damn good

to someone in that position, a dark part of my mind whispered. As soon as the thought surfaced, however, I shook it away.

Stop it. There's no way.

I looked back toward the fallen chair and saw the bottle of nail polish Elizabeth had left behind earlier. It wasn't all she'd forgotten. An entire pedicure kit lay nearby, its contents scattered across the rug: an oval piece of dark pumice, a pair of chrome clippers, some tweezers, and a metal fingernail file. I returned to the chair, kneeling beside it, trying to reach the file. It tapered to a point at the end, and I wondered if I could somehow use it to get out of the zip tie binding me.

I fumbled around on the floor behind me until I found the plastic handle of the nail file. I tried to turn it so I could poke at the clasp of the zip tie with the tip. If I could just wedge it somehow between the locking bar and the strip serrations, I might be able to disable it and pull it open. Of course, this was easier said than done, and since I didn't have eyes in the back of my head, the tip kept slipping and I jabbed myself in the wrist.

"Goddamn it," I muttered after the fourth or fifth time of cutting deep enough to draw blood. Then I opted to use the coarse side of the blade to try and file through the plastic strip, but after nearly dislocating my shoulder as I tried to crane my wrist at a good angle, I realized it would take way too fucking long to even bother. I could have hacked at them with the little set of nail clippers, but again, trying to maneuver them, and my arm, into the right angles proved next to impossible.

I returned to my original plan, and once again began repeatedly poking with the nail file, trying to pry open the locking mechanism. Just when I was about to give up in frustrated despair, I felt the tip of the file slide home, wedging beneath the lock bar of the zip tie. Before it could slip loose, I moved my hands apart. Instead of taut resistance, this time I felt the plastic strip give, sliding open. With a hoarse, shaky laugh, I jerked myself free.

Holy shit, I thought, clutching my wrist to my chest. My shoulders were on fire, my back and neck throbbing, my arms like overcooked spaghetti noodles, but goddamn it, I'd done it somehow.

I picked up the nail file again, then limped to my feet. After rechecking the entire room to confirm my wallet and phone were nowhere inside, I went to the bedroom door and squatted down, examining the lock.

It wasn't anything intricate, the kind you see in old houses all the time, with the distinctive keyhole through which countless horror movie characters would timidly peer, dreading whatever lurked on the other side. I didn't know the first thing about picking a lock, so I settled for shoving the nail file into the hole, then wrestling it back and forth, rattling the tumblers around. After a few minutes of this, I got pissed and started twisting it even harder. Just as the file snapped in my hand, breaking at the point where it met the plastic handle, I heard the lock obligingly click, the tumblers opening.

I stood, opened the door a few inches, then peeked out. Not sure why I felt the need to attempt discretion at that point, considering how much noise I'd just made forcing the lock open, but I erred on the side of caution as I looked first in one direction down the shadow-draped corridor, then the other.

To my left, at the end of the hall, I heard the faint sound of voices. Moving slowly, I followed the sound, but soon discovered the building I was in was laid out more like a maze than a home. One hallway branched into several others, then further divided from there, until I'd lost any and all sense of direction. Closed doors lined every corridor, and as I crept along, I paused now and then, trying different ones. Most were locked, with a few opening into shadow-filled rooms and unoccupied offices. None had any phones or computers I could find, nothing I could use to try and reach the outside world.

Eventually, I found a grand atrium. I was on an upper floor, the skylights directly overhead, the plain of the night visible through them. The voices were very loud now, along with the clinking of glassware, and the muted refrains of violin music. I crept close enough to the railing to get a look and saw what looked like a formal event underway several stories below. Dozens of guests were dressed in tuxedos and gowns, laughing and chatting as they sipped from flutes of champagne and nibbled hors d'oeurves.

What the fuck? When I heard Elizabeth's distinctive, shrieking laugh echo from somewhere within the gathering, I shrank back in bewildered alarm.

I didn't know what to do. Even though I could see an elevator on the other side of the atrium, along with a door marked as a stairwell, I wasn't sure if I should rush down to the party or not. True, there were people I could ask for help or to call the police. But then I thought about that night at the Brennus mansion, and how all the guests had seemed complicit when Robert carved a 'demonic symbol' into my back.

If these were the same people as before, or of a similar mindset, I knew I couldn't expect help from any of them. Instead, I hurried back down the corridor, away from the atrium.

At the end of another hallway, I found a pair of double doors. Beyond these appeared to be a library, with tall bookshelves lined with countless volumes of leather-bound tomes. Several glass-enclosed display tables had been arranged throughout the room, and with the curtains drawn back from the windows along the outer wall, enough moonlight filtered in to give them an eerie, unearthly glow.

Curious, I stole over to the nearest one, looking at the

objects on display. It was all a bunch of creepy shit: various skulls from what appeared to be birds, and severed claws that looked to be the same. Articles of jewelry had been placed among these: pendants, rings, and brooches, all adorned with a symbol—the now-familiar vertical line, flanked by a pair of triangles.

It's a winged figure, Traynor had told me. *A sigil.*

He'd been talking crazy, babbling about demons and how I'd been chosen, or some such bullshit. How that same mark had consecrated me somehow, whatever the fuck that meant. The same mark had been carved into trees around the Brennus mansion, Rodriguez had told me, near where they'd found each of the graves.

Were they planning to kill me, then? Some kind of fucking sacrifice?

I shuddered, glancing warily over my shoulder to be sure no one had followed me. Traynor had told me the name of the demon associated with that mark, but for the life of me, I couldn't remember what it was.

Something about how it has the body of a crow, I thought. *That's what the mark is supposed to represent.*

Looking into the case again, I realized the bird skulls were about the right size, and likewise, the disembodied talons were all black and leathery, like a raven's or a crow's.

This is fucked up. I crept over to the next display case. This one contained group photos of the Corvus Society members over the years, including several from the late 1800s, in which the Brennus mansion could be seen in the background. Several individual headshots were also on display, the founding members of the club: Allistair Brennus, Stephen Adler, Arthur Livingston, Oscar Ludwig, and Henry Mapother. Each portrait had a signet ring beside it emblazoned with the Corvus Society crest against a crimson garnet stone, with the words *Furca na alle laris* engraved on it.

As I turned away, a book on one of the nearby shelves caught my eye. Bound in dark leather, the spine had been etched in fading gold calligraphy that winked with reflected moonlight: *Codex Arcanum*.

The title sent another shudder through me.

Have you ever heard of the Codex Arcanum? Traynor had asked. *It's an ancient manuscript, a companion to the Lemegeton, known in our modern age as the Lesser Key of Solomon.*

"This is bullshit," I whispered as I reached for it, hooking it with my fingertip and sliding it slowly down from the shelf.

None of it's real. All that shit about demons, that was just Traynor blowing smoke up my ass. It's not real.

Still, I found my hand shook as I turned back the cover. It looked like a very old copy, the pages yellowed and brittle with age. It had been hand-scribed, row upon row of meticulously inked characters I couldn't read, a language I didn't recognize. Some of the characters didn't even look like part of the English alphabet.

I froze when I saw the heading: *Raum*.

The mark on your back—it's a winged figure, a sigil of Raum. Now I remembered what Traynor had said, the name of the demon he'd mentioned.

The great Earl of Hell, commander of thirty legions, the Night Demon...he appears to his acolytes in the form of a crow.

"Raum," I murmured, staring at the odd symbols, the different sigils and seals said to be used in Raum's summoning —including the one on my back.

You were marked in consecration, Traynor had warned. *I tried at first to give them Avery, but they turned me down cold. They wanted you, they said. Only you.*

The entry on Raum also contained illustrations of people killing goats, pigs, or rabbits in various rituals. One was labeled *Opes;* another *Vis.* Another, *Convocatio*, seemed to depict human sacrifices: five men standing at the vertices of a pentagram, their hands bound, while other men wearing masks slit their throats. The masks resembled the heads of birds, just like the plague masks Traynor and the others had worn at the Brennus mansion. Seeing this made my skin crawl uneasily, and I slapped the book shut.

I have to get out of here. Bullshit or not, something weird was going on, weird as fuck, and I had no desire or intention to stick around and see how it all played out. I left the book sitting on top of the case, then hurried toward the door. Just then, however, a woman breezed through the doorway, and had we both not skittered to startled, clumsy halts, we would've crashed into each other face-first.

"Oh my God," the woman exclaimed with a shaky laugh. "You scared the shit out of me. This place is like a maze! I'm trying to find the ladies...room..." Her voice faltered and she blinked at me. "Josh?"

I hadn't recognized her at first, not dressed like she was, in a coral floor-length dress with high neck and long sleeves. Her hair hung down over her shoulders in a tumble of ringlets, and she carried a little satin purse. She looked feminine and pretty, and it took my brain a bewildered moment to fill in the blanks and superimpose this image of her with the more familiar one in my mind.

"Ellis?" I gasped, and I couldn't have been shocked more shitless had she jumped into my arms and kissed me. "Wh-what the fuck...? What are you doing here?"

"It's a party." Her brows narrowed, her lips drawing together, and despite the makeover and cosmetics, she looked more like herself now, what I'd grown accustomed to. "I was invited."

I leaned over, looking past her toward the doorway. "Is Rodriguez with you?"

"He's running surveillance," Ellis said, frowning as she

reached up to tug at her ear. "Yeah, yeah, keep your pants on. I hear you."

I didn't understand what she was talking about until she lowered her hand, holding something she'd pulled from her ear: a small ear pod connected to a thin wire running up from beneath the edge of her collar.

"Put it in," she growled at me. "I'm mic'd up. He can hear you."

"What?" I grabbed the earpiece. The minute I slid it into place, I heard his voice.

"...you there?" Rodriguez said, sounding frantic. "Josh? Can you hear me?"

"I'm here," I said, nearly falling over in abject relief. "I can hear you."

"Thank God," Rodriguez said, his voice ragged. "I've been half out of my head. Are you alright? Did they hurt you?"

"No, I...I'm fine." Closing my eyes, I pressed my hand to my ear. "I'm sorry. I'm so sorry. I should've told you. I..."

"What? I can't hear you."

Ellis rolled her eyes, stepping closer, treacherously so. "The mic's here," she said, pointing to the neck of her gown.

"Oh." I leaned toward her, growing uncomfortably aware of her proximity thanks to the short tether of the earbud wire. For her benefit as much as Rodriguez's, I said, "I saw the other day, whenever you and Ellis came. They let me watch on some kind of security footage. I didn't kill anybody. And I never agreed to meet anyone from the Red Light District. I'd never do that, never fuck around for money, I swear. I'm sorry I didn't tell you," I added to Rodriguez, feeling my face blaze with shame. "About me, my livestreams..."

"Josh..." Rodriguez began.

"But I'd never do that. I swear to God, Rodriguez. I don't know what's going on. You have to help me! These people are crazy. They're some kind of demon-worshipping cult. They've got all these pictures and rings and shit with symbols on them, demonic symbols, Traynor told me. He told me they chose me. And I...I think..."

"Josh," Rodriguez said again. "Listen. Do you trust me?"

"I...I..." I sputtered. "Of course. Yeah."

"Good. Do me a favor and remember that, okay?"

"Wh-what?"

"Josh Finley, you're under arrest," Ellis said, snagging the earbud away from me. "For the murders of Antoine Sparks and Miles Pennington."

"*What?* But I...I already told you I don't know anything about them. I never—"

"You have the right to remain silent," she continued, snapping open her little handbag and pulling out a pair of handcuffs. "Anything you say can and will be used against you in a court of law. You have the right to an attorney..."

I backed away from her, bewildered and alarmed. "Wait," I said. "Stop. Let me talk to Rodriguez again."

"He can hear you through my mic," she replied coolly. "Do you understand your rights as I've explained them to you?"

"I didn't kill anyone!"

"Do you understand your rights, Josh?"

"The people here, they abducted me. They've been holding me against my will, drugging me, for Christ's sake, and you...you're arresting *me?* What the fuck?" Angry now, I held out my hand for the earbud. "Let me talk to Rodriguez."

"Put your hands behind your head. I'm going to place these handcuffs on you, then escort you to the nearest police station for questioning. If you resist, you'll face additional charges."

"You can't do that. Rodriguez, goddamn it, tell her she can't—"

"As I just said," Ellis told me, then, with sharp emphasis

on every word: "You are leaving this building with me right now, in my custody, and *no one can legally stop us.* Do you understand?"

Her words sunk in, or rather, the true meaning behind them.

"Do you understand?"

"Yes," I said, nodding. "I...I understand."

"Good. Put your hands behind your head."

Chapter 21

Ellis cuffed my hands in front of me, then marched me briskly through the web of corridors.

"What the hell is this place?" I asked.

"It's called the Brennus Building. Worldwide headquarters for the Corvus Society."

We reached an elevator, and she pushed the down arrow, looking around impatiently, as if making sure we weren't followed.

"There's a service entrance in the back," she said. "Through the kitchen. We'll go out that way."

The brushed chrome doors slid open, and I realized by the dingy interior, it was a service or staff elevator, rather than one meant for Society members or guests. Ellis jerked me into the car, then punched the button for the first floor.

"What if someone sees us?" I asked. "Tries to stop us?"

"I told you, they can't. You're under arrest."

"You don't really think I had anything to do with those murders, do you?" I asked, glancing over at her uncertainly.

"Do I think you committed them? Probably not. Do I think you have something to do with them? Probably so, whether you realize it or not. You said something about a cult, right?"

"Yes. People in the Corvus Society are part of it. Traynor was, too."

"There's a ritualistic appearance to the murders," she said. "Not just of the adults, but the children, too. The bodies were buried in very specific ways, in very specific positions."

"Where those marks are carved in the trees."

"Yeah," Ellis said, reaching into her purse again and pulling out a tube of lipstick. "I think they were used to designate the burial spots ahead of time. And if you plot them on a map, at least the ones we know about..."

She opened the lipstick, then dabbed it against the inside of the elevator door, leaving four marks. "...and then you connect them," she continued, drawing lines to intersect the points. "You can pretty much predict how many graves there will be altogether, and where the last one can be found in relation to the others."

"Five," I said, recalling what Traynor had told me. "There are five burial sites altogether."

"Arranged in a pentagram," Ellis said, as we reached the first floor and the elevator chimed again. "With the old Brennus mansion in the center."

I'd seen enough shitty horror movies in my life to know what a pentagram symbolized, what it meant. "What the hell do they want with me?"

"I don't know. But considering all the pains they've gone through to keep track of you over the years, it must be important."

Hooking me by the arm again, she led me off the elevator and down a service corridor.

"What are you talking about?" I asked.

"That website you like to jerk off on. It was developed by a man named Sigurd Gulbrandsen. He's a member of the

Corvus Society. He also owns a company called Datamaskin."

"What? My dad used to work there."

"Yeah, Gulbrandsen and Mapother are pretty tight. Their wives, too."

I felt my gut suddenly twist in a sickened, aching knot. Jesus Christ, had the Mapothers known about Easy Mark, then? Had they been watching me this whole time?

"Which explains how they could've set up your viewers to be victims," Ellis said. "Gulbrandsen probably has administrative access to your account. He could've sent messages to them, pretending to be you, arranging for meetings."

"But why? And why would he want to kill them?"

"I don't know. But like I said, it must be something important."

We reached a pair of swinging doors that led into a large industrial kitchen. Inside, uniformed staff hurried back and forth, carrying trays of dishes, food platters, and wine glasses. We caught a few curious glances as we cut through, but no one stopped or spoke to us.

"This way." Ellis led me to a back exit down a short, narrow corridor, one lined with stacks of boxes. A sign on the door said it was meant for emergency exits only, and that an alarm would sound if opened, but she reached for it anyway.

"May I ask where you're going, Agent Ellis?" Mapother said from behind us, his voice resonating over the collective din of the kitchen staff at work.

I turned, startled, and found him standing in the middle of the hall behind us, dressed in a well-tailored tuxedo with a single red rose boutonniere pinned to his lapel. The stark fluorescents overhead winked off something metallic in his hand: a pistol he held pointed at us.

"I hope you're not leaving us so soon," he lamented with an insincere frown.

"Yeah, well, to be honest, I'm getting bored," Ellis said, stepping forward, positioning herself in front of me. "You talk to one fat, middle-aged, balding guy with a bad combover and Courvoisier breath at these things, and you've pretty much talked to them all."

"I'm sorry to hear that. Of course, you're welcome to leave anytime. You can even use the front entrance. There's no need for all this trouble. However, that being said..." He narrowed his gaze at me. "I can't allow that young man to accompany you."

"Mr. Finley's under arrest. He's wanted in connection to a series of murders—ones that may have taken place on your property in Virginia. I found him wandering in one of the hallways while I was looking for a bathroom. I assume he broke in. Surely the Corvus Society hasn't been harboring a dangerous criminal here...?"

The corners of Mapother's mouth flicked up. "I'm grateful for your help, Agent Ellis, but again, I can't let him leave with you. You see, he's very...important."

"Why's that?" she asked, reaching behind her, her fingers brushing mine. I felt her press something into my hand, hidden from his view: the handcuff key, saw her mouth a single word as she glanced over her shoulder at me: *Run.*

Mapother's smile withered, his eyes glinting coldly. "He belongs to me."

"Run!" Ellis's hand darted into her purse again. She threw the satin bag aside, revealing a pistol she'd grabbed. Just as she moved to swing her arm up toward Mapother, he fired. The report of gunfire was sharp and booming in the narrow confines of the hall. The round hit Ellis in the upper chest, knocking her backwards, off her feet, her long skirt tangling around her legs as she swung in a clumsy pirouette. She crashed into a pile of boxes, scattering them, then crumpled to the floor, a bright red bloodstain already blooming across the bodice of her gown, just above her left breast.

"Ellis—!" I cried, scrambling to her side. When I looked back at Mapother, I saw the kitchen staff beyond him, all turned in our direction, eerily quiet now.

"Somebody call an ambulance!" I shouted, getting my arm beneath her shoulders, dragging her against my chest. She felt like deadweight, limp and lifeless, her head rocking back against the nook of my shoulder. Blood trailed from her mouth and nose, her hair hanging in her face.

"She's been shot!" Despite the urgency in my voice, the kitchen crew all stood there, looking at me, their faces stony and impassive. None of them said a word and nobody moved, like they'd all been hacked out of ice. "What the fuck's wrong with you people? Someone call a goddamn ambulance!"

Then, remembering Ellis was wired, I leaned over her, grabbing the collar of her dress. "Rodriguez, she's been shot! That crazy fuck shot—"

"Save your breath." I heard the ominous click of a pistol hammer drawing back and felt the cold press of a metal gun barrel against my temple.

"By the time they get here, we'll be long gone," Mapother continued coldly.

"You won't kill me," I said, glaring at him out of the corner of my eye.

He smirked. "You're right. But I can still shoot you...many, many times."

"Awww, you started without me," I heard Elizabeth say in a loud, grating whine as she walked around the corner. "No fair. You said I could kill that bitch."

"I aimed high. She's not dead yet."

"Don't touch her," I said as, with a vicious giggle, Elizabeth strolled toward us. "Don't fucking touch her, you—"

Mapother drove the stock of the pistol against the side of

my head, stunning the senses from me. I started to topple, but he grabbed a fistful of my hair, forcing me to stay upright.

"As for you..." he snarled, wrenching my head back. He'd passed the pistol to Elizabeth, and with his free hand, twisted my arm behind me, craning my shoulder at an agonizing angle. I cried out hoarsely as he slammed me into the wall and pinned me there, his lips brushing the edge of my ear as he spoke.

"I hope you enjoyed your little outing this evening, because I'm going to lock you away so deep in the bowels of this place, no one will ever find you, no matter how loud you scream. I'm going to chain you like a fucking dog and give you one bowl to piss in, another to eat from, and I'll strip every last scrap of hope you have of any sort of rescue or escape. I keep telling you, but now I'll make you understand, even if I have to carve it into every square inch of your fucking flesh. You belong to—"

The second gunshot came from somewhere behind me, so close that I glimpsed the bright flash as the round discharged. Blood splashed against the side of my head, dousing my face and hair. Moist chunks splattered across my cheek and the wall was suddenly drenched in violent, glistening red, like some kind of Jackson Pollock painting from hell.

At the same time, the crushing weight of Mapother's body fell away, his fingers slipping from my hair. He landed with a heavy thud on the floor, like a canvas sack of wet sand dropped from a second-story window. As I stumbled sideways, my ears ringing, I looked down and saw him sprawled by my feet, his head turned in profile, his eye open, his mouth hanging ajar. A pool of blood widened around him, and even from that angle, I could tell the other half of his face was all but missing, obliterated by the close-range gunshot.

"Oh, dear," I heard Elizabeth say with a titter. "I didn't let him finish monologuing."

I stared at her in confused horror as her husband's blood and brains dripped and pattered from my head.

She drew the pistol toward her mouth coquettishly, the way a Southern belle might try to hide behind a fan. "Whoops," she said, dropping me a wink.

I collapsed with a groan, my knees abandoning me, my mind shell-shocked. Elizabeth rushed forward, catching me.

"No, no, no," she said. "Not yet, little lamb. I need you to stay awake just a little longer." Hooking her arm around my waist, she steered me toward the back door. "Come on. I've got you."

As we moved past Ellis, who still lay on the floor, the bodice of her gown now soaked with blood, I heard her gasp feebly.

She's still alive!

She looked up at me, wide-eyed and terrified as she hiccupped for air, and in that split second as our eyes met, I realized we both understood the same thing: if Elizabeth noticed, she would kill her.

I groaned again, deliberately this time, and leaned so heavily against Elizabeth she had no choice but to focus on me, dragging me past Ellis without as much as a second glance. She shoved the back door open, then forced me across a concrete loading platform and down a short flight of steps toward a low-slung Mercedes coupe. She swung open the passenger door and shoved me inside. Leaning past me, she opened the glove compartment and took out a slim syringe, the needle covered with a plastic cap.

"No..." I groaned as she pushed my head, turning my face toward the steering wheel. "No, stop..."

I winced as the needle sank into my neck. Almost immediately, whatever she'd shot me up with hit my brain, that warm fog beginning to engulf me.

"What...did you give me?" I croaked when she flounced down in the driver's seat.

"Something to help you relax." Setting the gun in the console between us, she reached overhead, retrieving a set of keys from behind the sun visor. She fired up the engine, and the dashboard lights sprang to life, bright and blinding.

"Just sit back and close your eyes," she told me cheerfully, dropping the transmission into reverse. "Enjoy the ride."

WITHIN MINUTES, the drug hit me in full like a freight train, and I slumped in my seat, my forehead nodding against the window. I could see myself reflected in the glass, caked in drying blood and gore, but it felt like I saw it in a movie instead, like I'd detached from it somehow, and observed myself from a distance.

She turned on the radio, and R.E.M.'s "It's the End of the World as We Know It" blared out. Elizabeth began to sing along, mouth stretched wide in a maniacal grin, her husband's blood splattered on her face and neck.

Rodriguez... I thought, watching in a daze as lights streaked past the window. Had he heard everything through Ellis's mic? Did he know what had happened? Was he trying to find me?

I must have said his name aloud, because she switched the radio off and touched my blood-smeared face. I tried to pull away but couldn't seem to find the strength.

"Hush, now," she told me gently. "It will all be over soon."

"Wh...where are you...taking me...?"

"Home," she said simply, and as she stroked my hair, she began to sing: *"Hush you bye, don't you cry...go to sleep, little baby..."*

Chapter 22

"Do you know what *corvus* means?"

With a groan, I lifted my head. I had no clue how long I'd been out, but the lights of the city were gone, and outside the window there was only a dark-draped landscape speeding by, crowned with an infinite expanse of stars overhead.

I heard the rush of wind as she lowered her window an inch or two. From the corner of my eye, I saw a bright flare as she struck a lighter, then smelled smoke as she lit the tip of a cigarette she held between her lips.

"Do you?" she asked, glancing over at me, and, bewildered and dazed, I shook my head. "It's Latin. The genus for bird species which includes crows and ravens."

My mouth was sticky and parched inside. I felt the blood that had dried on my skin crack and crumble as I moved, straightening somewhat in my seat. My wrists were still cuffed together, and as my mind transitioned from out-cold to groggy awareness, I felt a momentary panic, remembering how Ellis had pressed the key into my hand earlier. I'd passed out, but managed to keep hold of it, could feel it now still resting against my palm.

"The Brennus family name means *crow*, too," Elizabeth continued. "I guess that's how all of this started. Allistair Brennus, Stephen Adler, Arthur Livingston, Oscar Ludwig, and Henry Mapother. They were the founding fathers. The ones who made the original pact."

"Pact?"

She nodded. "With Raum."

The demon Traynor had told me about, the one from the book I'd found in Mapother's library.

"I know this isn't going to make a whole lot of sense to you," Elizabeth continued, taking a drag of her cigarette, one of those ridiculously long and skinny brands that only women prefer. "But I'll try to explain. A long time ago, Allistair Brennus, Stephen Adler, Arthur Livingston, Oscar Ludwig, and Henry Mapother made a deal with a demon. It was right before the Civil War broke out, and it was obvious the country was going to shit, so they wanted some guarantee that no matter how things shook out in the end, they'd come out smelling like roses. You know what I mean?"

She glanced at me expectantly, huffing out a stream of smoke. I coughed, then shook my head.

"Why would *you* make a deal with the devil?" she asked. "Why would *anyone*? Deep down inside, when you strip away all the bullshit, we want the same things: money and power. Even when you have both, you still want more. So, that's what they asked for, why they sold their souls."

With a snicker, she held her cigarette up to the open crack of her window. Smoke, embers, and ash flew out into the night. "Well, not *their* souls," she amended. "They offered five sacrifices, one for each of them, plus one more, an anathema, they called it, a sacrifice specifically for Raum."

I remembered the drawings I'd seen in the book, the *Codex Arcanum*. One of them had shown five sacrifices, the victims standing in the shape of a pentagram. *Convocatio,* the ritual had been called.

"But here's the kicker. Raum agreed to give them what they wanted, but only on certain terms. The anathema had to be a son from one of their families. If a son was offered to him, and the other sacrifices were made, he'd grant their wishes for wealth and success, but only for as many years as the number of demon legions at his command—thirty. After thirty years, the ritual sacrifices have to take place again, and a new anathema offered in order to renew the pact."

Anathema. I recognized that word, too. Still, it made no sense. Elizabeth's words spun around in my mind.

"Confused yet?" she asked, then laughed. "Trust me, I know. The first time I heard all this, I thought it was bullshit, too. It gets better. So they all agreed to Raum's demands, and they all became rich and powerful in all kinds of industries. The Mapothers were lawyers and judges, the Brennuses became politicians, the Adlers hoteliers, and on and on. Anything they touched turned to gold, and all it cost them was a son every thirty years. And the sons of bitches eventually figured out a way around that, too, a loophole, I guess you could say, in their deal. Raum had only demanded a son. He hadn't specified a son *by blood*. So, if the anathema was adopted, the family wouldn't lose anyone from the bloodline. And that's what they did. The forms Raum has taken over the years since have all been adopted sons, ones who can only enjoy the privileges their sacrifices bought for thirty years—while the real, blood members of the families reap the true rewards."

Pinching her cigarette butt between her fingers, she sent it flying out of the window. A heavy silence, the sort that made my ears pop, fell between us as she closed her window again.

"Raum figured things out eventually, but since they'd made a pact, and technically hadn't broken it, he was bound by it. So, he found a loophole of his own. He started selecting the anathema in advance, when they were children. To keep the pact valid, they'd need to be adopted by one of the founding families. Only sometimes, Raum would then change his mind and pick someone else. And sometimes the kids he picked weren't up for adoption."

She glanced my way, looking ghoulish in her bloodstained evening gown, and even more so when she flashed me a predatory smile. "You don't remember, do you? Meeting Robert for the first time. You must've gone with your father to his office for some reason, because that's where he saw you. He was there to see Sig."

Did she mean Sigurd Gulbrandsen? Ellis said he owned the Red Light District website, and had been my father's old boss at Datamaskin. I'd only ever gone to see Dad there a handful of times, on afternoons when he'd pick me up from school and still have things left to do at work. I'd wind up sitting in a chair near the door of his office, facing his desk, reading manga or goofing around on my phone until he wrapped up whatever it was that had detained him.

"He told me when he saw you, he heard Raum speak, which almost never happens. Raum said he wanted you. Which was unfortunate because we'd already picked someone else to be the successor. But what Raum wants, Raum gets. We have to keep the cash cow happy, right?"

She spat those last words, her brows narrowed, her lips turned down as if in disgust.

"Do you know what happens to the anathema when Raum's finished with their body?" she asked me. "Apparently, he tears his way out, rips them open from the inside out. That's why Mapother and the others didn't want to give up their own flesh and blood. Not for that. And even though the anathema can get married, have kids, the whole nine yards, during their term, when their turn is up, what do you think happens? The wife and kids, they're not related by blood, so there's no need to keep them. Any of them."

She glanced at me again, and when she smiled this time, it looked strained. "We suffer 'unfortunate accidents,' if we're lucky. If we're not, we just disappear. They have ways of doing that, you know. The Corvus Society, I mean."

"Why are you telling me all this?" I asked.

"Because I think you have the right to know why this is happening to you, why everyone wants you. Your body, at any rate. As far as they're concerned, you're prime real estate. And you've been promised to a very important tenant."

"You mean..." I tried to wrap my head around what she'd said. It felt like trying to solve a Rubik's cube in the dark. "This thing...this demon, Raum, they want it to possess me? And if it does, then...what? It lives inside of me for thirty years and makes them all get richer?"

"And when it's done with you, it kills you." She reached for the center console, her pack of cigarettes again. "Pretty much, yeah."

"It picked me. It saw me one day and it picked me to possess. That's why Michael Traynor abducted me ten years ago. You told him to, gave him a promotion at his job to do it."

"The Corvus Society did," she corrected, lisping around the filter of a cigarette. "Yes."

"Why did they let me go, then? If I was so important, like you keep saying, why would they let me escape?"

"They didn't. Not the Corvus Society, anyway. Or Michael Traynor, either."

"Then who—" I didn't get the chance to finish, as something struck the front of the car, heavy and huge enough to shake the entire chassis, scaring the shit out of me and Elizabeth. For a wild moment, I thought we'd hit a deer in the road, then glimpsed a vaguely humanoid silhouette crouched on the hood, as if readying to leap through the windshield and attack.

Elizabeth shrieked, slamming on the brakes. Trying to go from 80-plus miles-per-hour to an abrupt dead halt went against the laws of both physics and inertia, and the tires screeched, the stink of rubber seared against asphalt filling the air. The Mercedes fishtailed before skidding to a stop, nearly sideways across the road.

I rocked forward, smacking face-first into the dash before rebounding again, snapped back by the strap of my seatbelt. I felt the handcuff key jar from my grasp and fumbled to keep a hold of it.

"What the fuck...?" I gasped.

Several large indentations buckled the hood, and steam curled out from beneath the crumpled edges, but there was no sign of whatever had hit us.

"What was that?" I asked, looking out through the windshield toward the shadow-draped woods beyond. The twin spears of Elizabeth's headlights seemed to hardly penetrate the dense growth at all.

"I...I don't know," she replied, breathless and clearly shaken. Clutching the gear shift, she dropped the car into reverse, then turned to look out the back window. I don't know if her foot slipped from the clutch to the gas, or if she meant to stomp on the pedal so hard, but the car whipped around in a smart semi-circle, the headlights swinging around to point down the empty highway. Again, she manhandled the gear shift, and the car lurched forward as she peeled out, leaving yet more skid marks along the pavement.

"Where the hell did it come from?" I asked. Whatever it had been, the damn thing sure hadn't run out in front of us like an animal; it seemed to have fallen on top of the hood, or, more precisely, pounced down onto it from somewhere above.

"I don't know." As she drove, her gaze kept darting from

the road to the car mirrors. She gripped the steering wheel tightly enough to blanch her knuckles.

"Where did it go?" Pivoting in my seat, I looked behind us, but saw only the empty road.

"How the fuck should I know? Stop asking so many—"

A tremendous thud shuddered through the entire car as something slammed into us, this time on the roof. Elizabeth shrieked, then again hit the brakes, bringing the car to a skidding stop in the middle of the road. I heard the scrape of knifepoints or claws across the paint above me, then something large and heavy crashed down onto the windshield, thrown forward by momentum, crushing the glass. I couldn't see much through the resulting cobweb of cracks and fissures zigzagging across the window, but felt the car shudder as whatever had rolled off the roof now tumbled onto the hood, then over the edge to the ground.

"Jesus," Elizabeth hiccupped. "Oh...oh, Jesus..."

A shadow moved in the swath of illumination cut across the road in front of us by the headlights. She didn't even give whatever was there the chance to get on its feet again. Wrestling the stick shift, the clutch grinding in protest, she stomped on the gas and the Mercedes lurched forward. I couldn't see anything through the busted windshield, and clearly, neither could she, because the car jostled violently as we ran over something large and unyielding. The next thing I knew, I could see the woods looming through the shards of broken glass as she veered toward them, out of control.

"Watch out—" I yelled. Elizabeth screamed, and the car hit a shallow drainage ditch by the shoulder of the road, then flipped. My seatbelt snapped taut again, biting into my neck as we lurched toward the driver's side, then upturned. For a split second, I felt the peculiar sensation of weightlessness as we went ass over elbows, then, with a jarring crash, we became earthbound again, landing upside down on the roof of the car. The engine continued running, smoke and steam spewing out from beneath the ruined hood, the headlight beams askance, one pointing off into the trees, the other into the dense, bare underbrush surrounding us. The windshield wipers had somehow come on, dragging across the splintered glass in erratic, spasmodic jerks. I could hear hissing coming from the busted radiator and smelled the pungent odor of gasoline.

Elizabeth blinked owlishly, her hair hanging down past her head, one of her glittery earrings now missing. Some of the blood on her face was fresh, streaming along the contours of her cheeks and nose toward her forehead from multiple lacerations.

Shit. When we'd flipped, the gun had tumbled around inside the car like a lone sock in a clothes dryer. Now it was nowhere to be seen. Elizabeth was dazed, hurt, and unarmed; I saw my chance to escape and decided to go for it. I still had the handcuff key, having clutched it so tightly in the rollover, you could've made a copy of it just from the imprint left behind in my palm. I drew my hands to my face and slipped the key between my teeth. Craning my wrist, I worked by the dim glow of the dash lights, fumbling until I got the key into the keyhole on the left cuff. I twisted the key and felt the bracelet release. I shook myself free of it, then reached for the second cuff.

"What...what are you...?" Elizabeth groaned, fumbling for her seatbelt latch. "Wait...you...you can't..."

"Fuck you," I seethed, releasing the second cuff. Seizing her by the hand, I slapped it closed around her wrist, and her eyes widened with sudden realization.

"No...!" she gasped, but it was too late; I locked the other cuff around the steering wheel. "No!"

As I unlocked my seatbelt, she pawed at my hands, scratching at me with her fingernails.

"You...can't leave me here," she cried, blood peppering from her lips.

"The hell I can't." I jerked myself loose, then scrambled out of the car. She tried to grab my legs, but I drove my heel back at her. "Get...*off!*" I cried hoarsely. "Get the fuck off me, you crazy fucking bitch!"

I kicked loose of her grasp, then army-crawled across the tangled carpet of dead grass, fallen leaves, broken limbs, and brambles until I was clear of her reach. My breath plumed around me in frosted huffs as I stumbled to my feet.

"You're crazy. All of you...fucking crazy. All that bullshit about demons, sacrifices, selling your souls..." It hurt to laugh, but I managed anyway, a coarse bark. "You're all out of your goddamn minds."

"Please," Elizabeth begged, her voice choked with tears as she reached for me, fingers splayed with desperation. "Please, don't—"

I heard a rustling from nearby, something unseen but close at hand, moving in the darkness. Something large. Elizabeth must have heard it, too, because all at once, her voice gulped short. We both strained to listen, then heard it again, closer this time. In the headlight beams, I could see the tips of tall, dried weeds waggle suddenly as something pushed through them, past them.

Elizabeth saw it, too, and began to wail. "Help! Oh, God, he's coming! Help me, please!"

A shadow rose from beyond the driver's side of the car, something towering enough to block out the moon. It looked vaguely human, at least at first, just like the thing we'd hit with the car. Then two elongated appendages spread out on either side of it, stretching as wide across as the length of the car, and more.

Are those...wings? I thought. *What the actual fuck...?*

From the outline of what I assumed to be the creature's head, two glowing slits of scarlet light appeared, then widened, like a pair of fiery eyes blazing out from the impenetrable dark. It uttered a piercing screech that punched into me like daggers and left me floundering backwards, crashing down on my ass, clapping my hands to my ears to try and muffle the horrific sound.

Elizabeth's scream overlapped it, and for a brief, terrifying moment, that hideous, winged thing looked at me, its red eyes impaling me, pinning me in place. Then it was gone, the entire silhouette collapsing as if it dropped to the ground on the other side of the car. Elizabeth's shrieks ripped up sharp, frantic octaves, then the entire car shuddered. Through the open passenger door, I could hear horrible things: ripping sounds, splatters, and growls. Elizabeth's wails hit a shrill crescendo, then abruptly fell silent, and I could only hear those wet, grinding noises, like claws through flesh and blood, or teeth gnashing, chewing...

"Oh...Jesus..." I couldn't see inside the car anymore; either the dash lights had gone out, or something enormous had forced its way inside and covered them up, but it didn't matter. The sounds were enough, and I clutched at my midriff as I retched into the grass, my gut twisting in an agonizing knot.

Get up, I told myself. *Get up, get up RIGHT NOW because whatever that fucking thing is, it'll come for you next, and you need to RUN.*

I limped to my feet and shambled toward the edge of the forest. My feet were bare, and I could feel rocks and thorny twigs digging into my soles, but I forced myself to run anyway, trying to put as much distance between us as possible while it was distracted inside the car.

I didn't make it far before I heard that godawful shriek from behind me again, echoing in the crisp, clear night air.

The hairs along the nape of my neck and forearms raised in renewed terror, and I pushed myself to run even faster.

Low-hanging branches whipped across my face, snagged in my hair, scraped my arms bloody. Moonlight filtered through the barren tree crowns to the forest floor, but it didn't make a difference. Not when everything looked exactly the same, no matter which way I turned.

I ran until my legs throbbed and my lungs burned with the desperate need for air. Panting, I fell against a tree trunk and struggled to catch my breath. By now, my T-shirt clung to my back with sweat, chilling me to the bone. My teeth rattled together, my entire body shaking. One at a time, I dared to lift my feet and grimaced at the blood left behind, glistening in the leaves beneath me.

From somewhere behind, something crashed through the forest. I froze, sucking in my breath, staring wide-eyed and terrified into the darkness. The sounds of pursuit faded to silence, but I knew it was only a momentary reprieve. This had happened several times already, enough for me to know damn good and well what that thing was doing.

It's fucking with me.

Even though I had no clue where it was hiding, judging by how close it had sounded, it probably knew exactly where to find me, and could catch up anytime it felt like. It was toying with me, like a cat with a hapless mouse, running it ragged until it collapsed with exhaustion.

Was it Raum? I didn't want to think that, didn't want to believe any of the Corvus Society or Elizabeth's bullshit. Still, I couldn't deny what I'd seen with my own eyes, heard with my own ears. Demons may be a bunch of bullshit, but whatever was after me was definitely real. My only chance was to somehow find help.

Ahead of me in the distance, I glimpsed a faint orange glow among the trees. Light could mean a house, or highway with passing cars, and I felt a surge of sudden hope. Shivering, aching, my feet battered and bleeding, I moved forward again, following that dim light, watching it grow brighter, larger, as I drew closer. The woods began to thin, and through the widening gaps between the trees, I could make out flames, and smelled smoke from what appeared to be a large bonfire.

Were people camping there? I forced myself to run again, clutching my side, trying to ward off a stitch beneath my ribs. As I neared the fire, I saw it had been built in a wide clearing, and toward the far side, I saw the orange glow of flames reflect against the façade of a large house, one I immediately recognized.

The Brennus mansion? I stumbled to a bewildered halt at the edge of the woods. Had this been where Elizabeth was taking me? There was no way it was a coincidence that I'd wound up here, but I had no idea why this would have been her destination, or who had built the enormous bonfire that now blazed in the front yard.

Before I could think too long or hard about it, I heard the snap-crackle-*POP* of leaves behind me—too close. I tried to bolt, not daring to glance over my shoulder, but something hooked my arm above the crook of my elbow, yanking me backwards. I sucked in a startled breath before a hand clamped over my mouth. I stumbled backwards into whoever had grabbed me, and when they craned my head back to their shoulder, I felt the hot rush of their breath against my ear as they whispered: "Stop."

A man's voice, low and hoarse. I struggled, trying to wrestle loose, but he tightened his grasp.

"Josh," he breathed, and my eyes flew wide again, this time in recognition. "Stop. It's me."

"Rodriguez?" I gasped, whirling to face him once he lifted his hand from my mouth. "Wh-what are you...?"

Emotions flooded through me, and I couldn't finish. I

rushed against him, hugging him fiercely. "You're here!" I exclaimed, my voice muffled by his jacket.

I felt him stiffen in reflexive surprise, then relax, slipping his arms around me. "Hey," he said gently.

"I'm sorry." I don't know what exactly I was apologizing for—there were too many things to count, I'm sure—but I felt I needed to say it at least a thousand more times.

"It's alright," he said, stroking my hair. I looked up at him and he kissed me. It was so damn cold, his mouth so warm. "Where's Elizabeth Mapother? I followed you from Baltimore. Once I figured out where she was going, I cut ahead and came around through the backwoods the way you and I did before."

"She's dead. I...I think so anyway. She crashed the car. Something hit us." I heard a rustle of leaves stirring somewhere close by, and turned, wide-eyed. "It followed me, chased me through the woods. I don't know what the fuck it is, but it's huge...!"

"Get behind me." Rodriguez reached beneath his jacket and pulled a pistol from his shoulder holster. I heard a soft metallic click as he thumbed off the safety, surveying the woods around us.

"What happened to Ellis?" I whispered. "Is...is she...?"

"First responders were arriving on scene when I took off after Mapother. She could still talk to me through the mic at that point, but..." He shook his head. "She's tough. She'll hold on, if only to spite me."

That sounded more like a wish than a conviction. "I'm sorry," I said, remembering the frightened look on her face, that horrible, hiccupping sound as she struggled to breathe. "This is all my fault."

"I don't see anything out there," he said, still studying the woods. "We need to cut back the way I came, get to my truck. Can you make it? Are you hurt?"

"I'm okay," I said, not a complete lie at the moment.

Between the surging adrenaline and the bitter fucking cold, I really wasn't feeling too much of anything.

"Here." Rodriguez shrugged off his jacket, then drew it around my shoulders. "Put this on. You'll freeze to death."

He touched my face, the dried blood and crusted gore, and I could see the frightened worry in his eyes.

"It's not mine," I mumbled, ducking away from his hand. "Not all of it anyway." As I slipped my arms into the sleeves, feeling the residual warmth of his body still lingering in the fleece lining, I glanced toward the tree line and the mansion beyond. "Did you start that fire?"

"What? No. Why on earth would..." His voice faded.

"Who did, then?" I whispered.

Rodriguez shook his head. "I don't—"

"Look at the house." I caught him by the arm and pointed.

The panels of plywood that had been used to cover any avenue of entry on the building had been removed. Reflected firelight danced across panes of broken glass in the windows, and the tarnished brass fixtures on the front door. We could see the outline of what remained of them within the bonfire, engulfed in flames.

"What the fuck?" I whispered.

"There's someone there," Rodriguez said, and through the leaping flames, I saw what he meant, the figure of a man visible as he stood on the other side of the blaze.

"Wait here," Rodriguez told me.

I caught a handful of his sleeve, drawing his gaze. "Fuck that."

"Stay behind me, then. Okay?"

I nodded, and we stepped out of the woods together, out into the clearing that surrounded the Brennus mansion. The fire was so huge and bright, we couldn't make out more than just that vague silhouette on the other side, but as we drew closer, moving between the blaze and the house, I realized.

"Rodriguez—" I gasped.

"I know," he said grimly, because he could see it, too: a man stripped down to his underpants, his body flabby and soft with age, his face hidden beneath a black leather plague mask. He'd been bound to a wooden post sticking upright from the ground, his arms behind him.

"Hey," Rodriguez called out. "I'm Special Agent John Rodriguez with the Federal Bureau of Investigation. Identify yourself."

The man moved at the sound of Rodriguez's voice, his legs twitching, the slight swell of his paunch heaving as he gasped. The elongated beak of his mask wavered, then lifted slowly. Any response he might have made was lost over the rush of the flames, the roar of the bonfire.

When we drew close enough, Rodriguez reached out, clasping the mask by the beak. The man stiffened, and this time, when Rodriguez identified himself, we heard muffled, frantic pleading sounds.

Rodriguez wrestled with the straps and buckles until at last he was able to loosen the mask. As he pulled it away from the man's head, I felt a surge of renewed alarm. What if it was another client from the Red Light District? What if, once the mask came free, he looked up at me and called me "Mark?"

"Wait—" I said, but it was too late. Rodriguez had removed the mask, letting it fall with a heavy plop to the ground. The man beneath hung his head as he strained for breath, his graying hair hanging down, obscuring his face.

"Thank..." he groaned. "Thank you..."

He lifted his head, squinting against the glare of firelight, his face flushed and greasy with sweat. I shrank back. It wasn't a client from the District after all, but someone else I knew—very well, in fact.

"Dad...?"

My father settled his bleary gaze on me. His eyes widened, his expression growing pained, as if seeing me there wasn't half the surprise for him as it had been for me.

"Josh," he croaked.

"Dad!" I rushed to him, trying to see how he'd been bound, how to undo the ropes around his midriff and wrists. "Jesus Christ, what...what's going on? Why are you—?"

The sharp report of gunfire ripped through the night, echoing across the clearing, bouncing back off the smooth surface of the dark lake nearby. I watched in stricken horror as Rodriguez flew forward, as if tackled by an invisible assailant from behind. He crashed to the ground, and I screamed his name, scrambling to his side and falling to my knees.

"Rodriguez," I cried again as I rolled him over, watching with a gruesome sense of déjà vu as a bloodstain spread against the pale fabric of his shirt in almost the exact same place where Ellis had been shot. "No, no...oh, Jesus...!"

I heard a strange metallic clacking from behind me, one I recognized only from video games and bad action movies: the ratcheting of a rifle, another bullet loading into position. The gunman approached us from the direction of the house, carrying a large bore rifle, his face momentarily obscured by the glare of the bonfire.

"Hey, man," he said, raising the gun to his shoulder, looking down the length of the barrel toward me. "You're out late. Or, let me guess: up early."

"Paul?" I whispered, so stunned, I fell back onto my ass, staring at him in disbelief. "Wh-what...what the fuck...?"

"Josh." Rodriguez seized my hand and stared up at me, pleading. "Run...!"

"Where's Elizabeth?" Paul asked, still aiming at my head. I couldn't think straight, couldn't move, couldn't even seem to breathe, and sat there, stricken, gulping for air like a polliwog that's made landfall. When I didn't answer, his brows narrowed. "I'll ask you one more time. Where is Elizabeth?"

"She...she's dead. There was a car wreck. Something attacked us. It...it got her..."

He seemed to process this for a moment, then shifted one shoulder in a shrug. "Well, damn. That's too bad. She was good in bed...for an old lady, I mean. And she sure did love your dog."

"Wh-what?" I said, but then the cogs in my brain turned and fell into place.

Like I want to walk in on you getting busy with what's-her-name, I remembered joking with him, to which he'd replied:

Beth. And she's out of town, went to Chicago or something like that.

She's been in heaven, he'd told me after dog-sitting for Lucy. *Beth took her to the dog park earlier, and look, she painted her toenails.*

"Beth," I whispered. Short for Elizabeth.

"We had big plans, the two of us," Paul said. "But I guess it doesn't matter. I'd put all this together long before she came on board."

"What are you talking about? You...you're my friend, Paul. Why would you—"

"My name's not Paul. You really are a stupid fuck, aren't you? I can't believe you haven't figured it out yet."

"Wh-what?" I said, then looked at him—really looked at his face, his smile, like the fake, painted-on smile of a doll.

And I realized.

"You're Avery Ormsby."

"Bingo! Took you long enough. Jesus Christ, I thought I'd have to spell it out for you in big fucking block letters or something." The barrel of the rifle had drooped as he spoke, but he hefted it again, pointing at me, his eyes glinting. "I'm the one who should've been chosen—the one who *was* chosen, at least until you came along. You stole my chance, you son of a bitch. You stole my fucking life."

"Wh-what? I didn't steal anything from you. I never—"

He fired the gun, striking the ground inches away from my feet, kicking up a spray of dirt clots and leaf bits. I scrambled back, drawing my arm up to shield my face.

"Traynor took me first," he shouted, spittle flying from his lips, glistening in the firelight. "He told me I was special. I was chosen, he said, to be the anathema, the Night Demon's next vessel. I'd have anything I ever wanted, that's what he said. He promised it to me—anything I wanted!"

"He lied," I said. "The anathema isn't special. It's just another sacrifice, someone those rich fucks pick out to die, because they don't want to lose any of their own precious family. They keep you alive for thirty years, then they murder you, all because of some bullshit story about devil worshipping."

"It's not the devil you're promised to," Paul said. "It's Raum. And thirty years of luxury beats the fuck out of a lifetime of being poor, working for chump change, pouring beers for worthless fucks like you at all hours of the goddamn night."

I stared at him, dismayed.

"I was chosen first," Paul snapped. "Raum's supposed to be with me. Beth believed that, too. She told me what I need to do to fix things."

"Fix...?"

"Raum's been bound to this cycle because the Corvus Society forces him to it every time they repeat the *Convocatio*, the summoning ritual. To break that cycle and set Raum free, I need to complete the ritual on my own. Then he'll be bound to me, and all the wealth and power the founding families have enjoyed will belong to me, too. All I need is one more body to complete the *Convocatio*, a final sacrifice offered in his name. It was supposed to be that fat fuck who's always fawning over you in your livestream, what's his name? Gordon Stansbury."

Gordon? I thought, horrified. I'd never known his last name.

"He was in Annapolis, and God, I bet he about shit his pants when I signed in as you, told him you wanted him to fuck your brains out in person. He was even stupider than you if that's possible."

"Where is he?" I asked, understanding now how the other victims Rodriguez and Ellis had found had come from the Red Light District. Paul had been tricking them all along, using my account without me realizing. "What did you do to him?"

"Nothing. I mean, I was going to, but then Robert Mapother got his panties in a knot, locked you up where I couldn't get to you. At least not right away. And without you, there's no point in trying to summon Raum, is there? Not while he's bound to you, anyway. The only way to set him free is to remove any mortal attachments. So, while we were waiting for Beth to spring you, your boy Gordon decided to throw a clot or something, had a fucking heart attack, keeled over dead as a fucking doornail."

His smile stretched wide as he dropped me a wink. "Can't really sacrifice someone who's already dead, am I right? Lucky for me, your old man's stupid, too. I called him up, told him I knew where you were, that you needed help, and he came running, no questions asked. Both of you, dumb as fucking rocks."

"Stop," I said, holding up my hands. "Please, Paul, just stop."

"Come on, man. I'm doing you a favor. You know he sold you to them, right? Just like my old man sold me. They flashed money in his face, and he signed on the dotted line—his own flesh and blood."

I couldn't bite back a low, hurt groan at this, because that idea had been with me for some time now, the sickening, painful realization that my own father had known about this all along, even before I'd been abducted.

"No," Dad said from behind me, his voice strained. "No, oh, God, Josh, that isn't true. Listen to me. I never—"

"Liar!" Paul shouted, and the next rifle shot blew a golf-ball-sized hole in the wooden beam above Dad's head, showering him with splinters. "You goddamn liar! I know the truth, and so does Josh. Look at him. Look at what you did to your son!"

Dad hung his head, his hair drooping into his face. For a long moment, he remained like that, silent and unmoving, but then his shoulders twitched, he started to tremble, and I heard him utter a choked, sodden sound, like a sob.

"I'm sorry," he said, and it felt like someone had just shoved a knife between my ribs, sinking the blade into my heart. It was one thing to think about shit like that, imagine it in your mind, but another thing altogether to hear the admittance aloud.

"I'm sorry, Josh," Dad said, looking up at me, weeping. "I...I'm so sorry."

Paul laughed, a triumphant whoop. "You see? He admits to it! He sold you like a goddamn slave!"

"N-no," Dad cried. "No, that's not true. They came to me when I worked at Datamaskin, told me what they wanted, how much they were willing to pay. I was horrified. I turned them down—handed in my resignation that very same day."

"What?" I whispered.

"I couldn't go to the police. These men are powerful. You have no idea. And I...I foolishly thought if I quit, they'd leave you alone, forget about you. But they didn't. And then they... they took you..."

His voice broke, dissolving into an agonized cry, and his entire body shuddered from the force of his sobs.

"They took you," he wept. "And all I could think was it was my fault, because I couldn't stop them...couldn't protect you..." His body sagged against his bonds, his head lowering again. "Then you were back. I didn't understand why...how you'd escaped, but you didn't remember anything and I...I couldn't ever tell you the truth. I'm so sorry. Please forgive me."

"You escaped because of me, Josh," Paul said. "Not the police. Not your piece-of-shit father here, or some miraculous act of God. *I* let you out of the basement where Traynor kept you. *I* unlocked the front door so you could get away. I'm the one who did it, because I thought they'd choose me if you weren't around. If you were gone, then they'd want me again."

His expression had grown child-like, wounded and forlorn, but abruptly hardened again, his brows furrowing, his lips twisting into a sneer.

"But they didn't," he spat. "They only wanted you more after that, because they couldn't have you. Then Traynor got caught and sent to prison. He was the only one who loved me, who thought I was special. He was more of a father to me than my shitbag old man had ever been, and he was gone—because of *you*."

"That wasn't love," I said, stricken. "Traynor...he abused you."

"You don't know," Paul shouted, swinging the gun in my direction. "You don't know shit because you forgot it all. You and your amnesia—I know the fucking truth! I know Traynor loved me! I was doing this for him, so we could be together. I'd offer the sacrifices, set you up for the murders. I make the pact with Raum, and Traynor gets released from prison just in time for you to go in. If you didn't get the chair for five murders, you'd at least get life. And maybe, if you were lucky, you'd last a day without getting gang-banged, a full twelve hours before someone—"

"Fuck you," I screamed at him. "I thought you were my friend! I...I trusted you!" Choked for breath, nearly hyperventilating, I doubled over, tears streaming down my face.

"Josh..." Rodriguez said softly. His hand moved weakly, reaching out, lighting against mine long enough to get my attention.

"I..." I hiccupped, strangling. "Rodriguez, I...I'm sorry...!"

"Breathe," he whispered, somehow managing to smile, even as blood trailed from the corner of his mouth down his chin. "Breathe...for me, Josh."

"I can't."

"Yes, you can. Come on...big breath in. Everything's... okay."

I shook my head, because it wasn't okay. Everything was completely fucked, and it was all my fault.

"Three things," Rodriguez wheezed. "Tell me...three things you can see. Look around...and tell me..."

"I...I see you. Your...annoying...fucking face."

He tried to laugh, but winced with pain. "What else?"

I glanced around, then saw his pistol lying nearby. It had fallen from his grasp when he'd been shot.

My eyes flew wide, realizing that's what he wanted me to see, what he'd meant for me to find. As our gazes met, he nodded once in unspoken imperative.

"Alright, Josh," Paul said. "It's reckoning time. Who would you like to lose first, your father or your boyfriend? I'm afraid they've both got to go, but I'll let you decide who you want to hang onto the longest, if only by a few extra minutes." He made a show of checking his watch. "You've got thirty seconds to decide."

"Wh-what? No. You son of a bitch, no!"

"Twenty-three seconds."

"Josh," Rodriguez said, clasping my hand again. "Do it... now..."

"Kill me," Dad said to Paul. "Shoot me if you want...but please...please don't hurt my son."

"Fifteen seconds," Paul said, then in a mocking, sing-song voice: "Eeny, meeny, miny, moe. Who will be the first to go?"

"You don't have to do this," I said. "Any of it, Paul. We're both victims. They did this to us—the Corvus Society. We can choose to stop it."

As I spoke, I reached for the gun, leaning over Rodriguez and angling my body to disguise my movements.

"Right here," I told Paul. "Right now. Let's just stop it. Please."

My fingers brushed against the side of the pistol, and I curled them around the grip. I'd never fired a gun in my entire life, had no idea what the fuck I was doing, but Rodriguez needed me. He was counting on me, and as many times as he'd been there for me, helped me, I wasn't about to let him down.

"Five seconds," Paul said, unmoved by my pleas. "Four... three..."

"Paul, goddamn it—"

"...two..."

"—just stop!" I started to shout, but the cry died in the back of my throat as in front of me, through the wall of bonfire flames, a towering figure suddenly emerged. At least seven feet tall, with shoulders as broad as a Freightliner's grill, there was no way in hell it could be anything human. From behind that same wide expanse, a pair of wings slowly unfurled, stretching out, alight with flames. It had feet like talons, enormous, twisted claws, and from its head, the same two blood-red eyes I'd seen outside of Elizabeth's car bored across the clearing, straight into me.

Paul saw it, too, and ridiculously, he began to laugh, his mouth spread in a wide, gleeful grin.

"He's here," he screeched. "The great Earl of Hell, commander of thirty legions—the Night Demon has arrived! Lord Raum, I summon you. I beseech you! I invoke you!"

He began calling out in a language I didn't understand, words that sounded more like guttural growls and cries than any semblance of vocabulary. As he spoke, the creature hesitated, still engulfed in flames, its gaze fixed with unwavering focus on me.

"Now is the time," Paul shouted. "The circle is almost complete, the ritual about to be concluded. You'll be free to choose a new master, and I beseech you, let it be me! I summon you, oh Lord Raum! I invoke you!"

He swung the rifle toward my father, the only clear shot he had, given I was blocking his aim at Rodriguez. Everything seemed to move in excruciating slow motion all at once. I lifted Rodriguez's gun, tightening my grip on the stock, sliding my finger against the trigger. As I moved, Rodriguez sat up, his arms encircling me from behind, his hands clasping over my own.

"Just breathe," he whispered against my ear, helping me aim, holding me steady as I squeezed the trigger and fired. The recoil shuddered through my arm, up to my shoulder, knocking me into him, but he kept me from falling, one hand moving from the gun to my stomach, bracing me against him.

The bullet hit Paul in the chest, plowing him backwards. He hit the ground, legs splayed, the rifle bouncing out of his grasp. For a moment, he lay still, then he began to move, pushing himself into a half-seated posture, leaning heavily to the side.

"You..." he croaked, lifting one hand feebly, arm shaking as he reached out. The front of his coat now had a large hole blasted into it, and down lining fluttered in the air around him like snow flurries. No blood had seeped through, not yet anyway, but as he spoke, it burbled between his lips, spilling down his chin in a glistening, gory torrent.

"You...piece of...shit..." he hissed, glaring across the clearing at me. When his gaze fell across Raum, however, his expression softened, his brows lifting in what could only be described as rapture.

"My lord," he whispered, then he crumpled back to the ground, his hand dropping limply, heavily, his body lying still.

For a long moment, there was nothing but the roar of the flames, the snapping and crackling of burning wood, the whistle and hiss of embers. Then Raum moved toward me, its enormous talons tearing deep gouges in the earth with each step. Its body remained on fire, its wings stretched wide, those horrible eyes fixed on me.

"No...!" I gasped, shrinking back.

"You...can't have him," Rodriguez seethed. Twisting the gun from my hand, he pushed me behind him, then began shooting as Raum approached. "I said you can't have him!" Again and again, he fired, each of the bullets disintegrating with a flash of light, seeming to melt instantly from the heat as they struck Raum's chest.

"You can't have him!" Rodriguez cried again, still shooting. *"Vete a la chingada*—I'll never let you have him!"

Raum came to a stop less than five feet from us, so close, I could smell the stink of sulfur as its body burned, feel the heat radiating from it in waves. It threw back its head, and a fiery maw gaped wide, its mouth opening as it uttered a shrill, hideous shriek. I could feel that cry ricocheting inside my skull, cutting through my brain, and clapped my hands over my ears, trying to block it out.

Rodriguez fired once more, his last shot striking the creature in the head, sending a shockwave through the massive form. Whatever fuel had maintained that molten, impossible heat abruptly extinguished. The flames snuffed out, the fire diminishing, leaving only a charred husk behind. It remained standing only a fraction of a second before disintegrating altogether, blown into a sudden, rushing cloud of ashes that the wind buffeted around us in all directions.

Rodriguez fell against me, shielding us both from the ash storm. When at last the air began to clear, I dared to lift my head, half-expecting to see Raum had returned, its seeming demise only a bluff, or that Paul had somehow survived and reclaimed his gun, that he'd be standing there, aiming for me, his finger flexing against the trigger.

But there was nothing except the dwindling remains of the bonfire, the last of the plywood panels collapsing together like a fallen house of cards, sending a spray of red-hot embers spiraling skyward in a bright array.

"Josh..." Rodriguez groaned, slumping toward the ground. I caught him in my arms, and God, he looked bad, his skin unnaturally pale, his eyes glassy and dazed. He'd felt so warm to me only a short time ago, but now, despite our proximity to the fire, his skin felt cold.

"Rodriguez," I gasped, laying him on his back as gently as I could. Clutching his hand, I leaned over him. "Hey, man. You did it. You...you saved us."

I began to cry, my tears falling onto his face like raindrops. Once I started, I couldn't stop, as if ten years' worth of repressed, unbidden emotions suddenly came to a head inside of me, bursting free. He touched my face again and I sobbed, clutching at his hand.

"Please don't go," I begged him. "Please...!"

"It's...alright," he murmured.

"I want to be with you," I whispered, looking down at him through a veil of tears. "I need you. Please stay with me."

His eyelids fluttered closed, his smile softening. "I...I'm not going...anywhere..."

Chapter 23

Long story short: I managed to untie Dad, and between the two of us, we half-carried, half-dragged Rodriguez back through the woods to where he'd left his truck. At this point, I was operating in the same fugue state the police had found me in the night I'd escaped from Traynor's house—or rather, the night Paul (or Avery), had set me free, my brain too shell-shocked to do much more than run standard operating procedures: breathe, blink, move.

Dad drove us to a hospital, though I'm still not entirely sure where. I spent the ride in the back seat of the SUV, cradling Rodriguez's head in my lap, crying like a dumbass, because whatever dam in me had burst back at the Brennus mansion must have been holding back Lake Michigan in terms of emotions. I don't remember much about the long car ride out of the woods, except keeping my hands pushed against Rodriguez's chest, where the bullet had punched clean through him, trying to slow his blood loss.

One STAT MedEvac flight, three surgeries, and a month-long stint in the ICU later, and Rodriguez was released home. Two weeks after that, he was back at the FBI full-time. Apparently, binge-watching true crime shows on Netflix only made him long to be back in the field.

Ellis didn't die, either, as she's fond of pointing out. "A silver bullet couldn't kill me," she told me once with what probably constituted—at least for her—a friendly punch in the arm. She did, however, opt for a lighter duty appointment rather than return to fieldwork because, as she put it, "I'm getting too old for this shit."

My father hadn't been lying when he'd said the Corvus Society was made up of powerful people. The entire incident at the Brennus Building had been glossed over in the media. The same was true for the death of Elizabeth Mapother, save for a short mention in the Society section of the *Post* online about her succumbing to a brief illness.

Robert Mapother's untimely demise, however, was never made public, at least to my knowledge. Then again, it's not like I followed the D.C. celebrity gossip circles before any of this happened, and I sure as hell didn't in the aftermath.

In fact, once Rodriguez had been released from the hospital, I tried to put as much of the whole experience behind me as possible. Things between Dad and me got better. Whenever I'm in town, we get together and watch the Ravens play, or have dinner and all that happy horse shit. You know, like a real family, as Bree says—Rodriguez included. He and Dad share an adulation of the Ravens that borders on lunacy, so they've really bonded over that. And neither Mom nor Dad freaked out like I feared they would when I told them I was gay. By that point, if that night at the Brennus mansion hadn't clued my dad in, nothing was going to, but Mom took it pretty much in stride, too. Which means yet again, Bree enjoyed a hearty "I told you so" moment at my expense.

It meant a lot to Rodriguez, too, as it turns out. He eventually confided that he'd told his own parents about being gay a few months before his father's death. "My father was furious," he told me. "I've never seen him so angry, not in my entire life. He told me he was ashamed of me. He raised me better, he said."

They hadn't spoken after that, never had the chance to patch things up, and I think that's why he goes out of his way to spend time with my dad. He's making up for the time he lost with his own.

I stopped doing livestreams, but thanks to the technical skill set I gained, I was able to land different remote video production and editing gigs that eventually allowed me to quit the package warehouse. I started working from home, which meant I could maintain my carefully laid façade as an introverted recluse, at least until Rodriguez coaxed me out of the house for the occasional pitcher of margaritas and tequila shots.

It was over these aforementioned tequila shots one night, about a year after everything had gone down, that Rodriguez told me he'd been offered another position within the Bureau.

"It's with the crimes-against-children division of the Behavioral Analysis Unit," he said, which was the equivalent of Greek to me, but I raised my shot glass in his honor, nonetheless.

"That's fantastic, man," I said. "You get a raise out of it, too?"

I meant to make him laugh. Normally, he would have. But that night, he only smiled, not his usual sort, but something melancholy. "And a moving stipend."

"Moving...?"

"It's in Quantico. In Virginia."

"Oh," I said carefully. "How...uh, far is that?"

"About two hours," he said, and I struggled not to let it show on my face, that distinct feeling of having been drop-kicked in the balls.

"That's not so bad," I remarked lightly, filching his shot

glass, and knocking it back. No salt, no lime, just that sudden bitch-slap of tequila.

He'd said it first, not too long before that night, as a matter of fact. After we'd finished having sex, Lucy had grown impatient and scratched on my bedroom door, wanting to come in. I'd fussed at her to try and chase her off, then thrown my pillow at the door, but it hadn't worked.

"She's jealous," Rodriguez said with a chuckle.

"Yeah. I'm taking up her place in bed with you," I growled, pushing the covers back and sitting up.

That's when he said it. He caught me by the hand, stopping me on the side of the bed.

"I love you, Josh."

I sat there, frozen in the dark, acutely aware of the warmth of his hand against my skin. "I love you, too."

"Come with me to Quantico," he said that night over shots at Encanto.

"Sure." I gave a nonchalant shrug, even though when he said this, it made my heart flutter in that stupid, happy, helpless way it had when he'd told me he loved me. "I mean, on the weekends, at least. Bree could watch Lucy, and—"

"I mean, come with me," he said, reaching across the table, taking me by the hand. "Move with me. Be with me."

Of course, I'd known all along that's what he meant, but it still made me smile.

"I don't know." I shrugged again, and this time he laughed. "What? I've got shit to do. I can't just up and drop it all. I have a life, you know."

Which was bullshit, because my life was right there in front of me, holding my hand, grinning at me in that goddamn annoying frat-boy way he had.

And he knew that, too.

FIVE YEARS LATER, I woke up at six o'clock one morning in late November and took Lucy outside. The condo in Quantico where Rodriguez and I lived had a walk-out patio on the first floor that opened onto a fenced backyard, and this made things a lot easier for Lucy now that she was technically a senior citizen in dog years. She couldn't navigate stairs well anymore due to arthritis, and she moved everywhere at a snail's pace, stopping every few shuffling steps to sniff the grass. I guess it's a holdover from our time in the city, when she'd grown accustomed to smelling dozens of other people and dogs all around her.

"For fuck's sake, it's your yard," I told her for at least the bazillionth time since we'd moved there. "No one else has been out here but you."

It was dark and cold, and I didn't feel like standing out there, freezing my nuts off while she poked at every weed. Leaving the outside light on to help guide her back to the door —because her eyesight, as well as her hearing, had grown as feeble as her joints—I went into the kitchen and started a pot of coffee.

As it brewed, I poked around in the refrigerator and pulled out a carton of eggs. While I whipped several into a froth in a measuring cup, I glanced out the window and watched Lucy continue her investigation along the outermost edge of the security lamp's glow.

"Silly dog." I knew she would have to be put down sooner rather than later, before her ailments became more than we could manage, and it hurt my heart.

I made scrambled eggs, because that's still all I know how to cook with any proficiency. Fortunately, Rodriguez is chef enough for the both of us, so eggs and a couple of slices of toast are all I'm ever called upon to produce.

As I leaned down, scooping part of the eggs into Lucy's

food bowl, I heard Rodriguez come into the kitchen behind me.

"You're up early," he remarked.

"I've got an eight o'clock Zoom meeting with Greta."

"Oh." He snagged a mug out of one of the cabinets, then poured himself some coffee. I pulled a pair of forks from the dish drain beside the sink and handed him one. We stood together, me holding the pan between us, and ate scrambled eggs.

"You could try putting cheese in these, you know," he suggested.

"Look who's bitching about the free breakfast someone made for him," I said, making him laugh. "Made with love, at that."

"I'm an asshole."

"You said it, not me."

He took his toast to go and left me holding his half-empty cup of coffee. When he kissed me, it occurred to me—not for the first time—that I would never get tired of this, of being with him, of his hands and mouth touching me.

"Love you," he said, heading for the front door. "See you tonight."

"Yeah, if you're lucky."

Lucy still hadn't come inside, so I leaned out the patio door and called to her. I could make her out on the far side of the yard; the sun had risen just enough by now to cast a dim, rose-colored glow. She didn't look up when I hollered, but then again, she was mostly deaf, and since I didn't feel like plodding through the cold, damp grass to chase her down, I decided to let her do her thing a while longer.

I topped off Rodriguez's coffee and took it into the adjoining dining room, which I'd converted into my office. I fired up my computer and for the next hour or so, worked on several ongoing projects in my queue. I checked my email, reviewed my Outlook calendar, and polished off three coffee refills by the time the Zoom meeting with Greta Skarsgård, my manager, was scheduled. Even though she lived in Sacramento, and was three hours behind me, I found her waiting for me online when I logged on.

"Jesus. Don't you ever sleep?"

She laughed through her webcam. "I'll sleep when I'm dead. Too much to do in the meantime."

We talked shop for a while, and I filled her in on the status of my various assignments. She updated me on some deadline changes and schedule amendments, then explained they'd had to re-record some soundtracks for some clips I was working on.

"I'll send you the updated files today," she told me.

"Sounds good."

The doorbell rang, surprising me. Rodriguez and I never had visitors, because we didn't really do much other than hang out, just the two of us. I don't know if it's because he wasn't much of a social butterfly before he met me, or if my reclusive habits had rubbed off on him. In any case, I couldn't fathom why anyone would visit that early.

"Hang on a sec," I told Greta, pushing my chair back from the desk.

Curiously, I found a delivery waiting for me on the front porch: a large basket wrapped in cellophane with a large red bow at the top.

"What the fuck?" As I carried the basket inside, Greta must have caught sight of me as I brought it past my webcam because she called out.

"Woah, what's that?"

"Beats me," I said, carrying it over to my desk to show her. "Looks like muffins."

"Oo, a secret admirer, perhaps?"

Tucked under the ribbon, I found a small white envelope

containing a little card. As I read it, I glanced up at the camera and found her grinning impishly at me.

"Told ya," she said with a wink.

"You didn't have to do this."

"I know. But the Ad-Voidance account was a big win for the firm. And we couldn't have nailed it without you. I wanted to show you some appreciation."

"You couldn't just give me a raise?"

"Try one. They're from a local bakery near there. One of my friends recommended it to me. She said they're world-famous."

"World-famous, huh?" I said dubiously, unfastening the bow. "How's that happen? Did a Kardashian eat one or something?"

Greta laughed, watching as I peeled back the outer plastic. The aroma of buttery, sugary goodness wafted out, and I dipped my hand inside the basket.

"So, which kind is famous?" I asked. "You sent a shit-ton here. I don't want to waste my time with some average, subpar muffin."

"Quit being a dick. They're all supposed to be good."

"I'm taking you at your word," I said, plucking one out. It came swaddled in a square of tissue paper to keep you from getting your fingers sticky. "I think this one's blueberry."

"Those are my favorite. I'm on a keto diet. Eat a bite for me."

I tore the muffin in half, careful not to drop crumbs on my keyboard. Knowing Greta was watching, I took a wolfish bite in front of my webcam, making a show of savoring it.

"Holy shit," I said, only with a mouthful of muffin, it came out: *Hoe-wee thip!* I rolled my eyes, then slumped back in my chair, moaning.

"You are such an asshole."

"I can't help it," I told her. "It's so good. I can see why it's world-famous now. This is better than sex. I'm serious. I'm this close to shooting off in my pants as we speak."

To make her laugh even more, I stuffed the entire muffin in my mouth. Which made me laugh, too, until I started choking.

"Goddamn it," I said. "I spit crumbs everywhere."

"Serves you right. Come on. Let's wrap this up."

We reviewed some more production details together, then out of the blue, she asked me, "What do you think of Ryan Turner?"

Puzzled, I shrugged. "I hardly know the guy."

He was another remote editor with the company, relatively new to the role. We'd talked a handful of times over Zoom and had shot each other a couple of emails, tops.

"I'm just concerned he won't be able to handle the whole Diadem account on his own," she said.

"He doesn't have to. I'm working on it, too, remember?"

"Yeah, but I mean, once you're gone."

I laughed. "What? I'm not going anywhere."

"Of course you are."

She looked surprised, if not genuinely puzzled, which made me stop laughing and wonder what the fuck she was talking about.

"It's almost time, Josh. Don't you remember?"

"Time for what?"

"For the *Convocatio*."

I stared at my computer screen, her face in full view. My mouth suddenly felt tacky and dry, my throat tightening. It had been a long time since I'd had a panic attack, years since I'd last let my anxiety get the better of me or had to take any of my pills. Yet now, I could feel my heartbeat quickening, my stomach twisting into an uneasy knot.

"What..." I said, my voice hoarse and warbling. "What are you talking about?"

Greta smiled at me. "The *Convocatio*. It will have been thirty years soon. The Great Earl is waiting to claim you."

"What?" I pushed my chair away from the desk, then staggered to my feet.

No, I thought, in frightened dismay. *No, no, this can't be happening. It's all over now. We stopped it. Rodriguez helped me stop it!*

"We're all waiting for you here," Greta told me, and her camera zoomed back, the space behind her spreading into view. I recognized her surroundings, the bookshelves and glass cases—not California at all, but the library at the Brennus Building. Dozens of people had gathered behind her, more than could fit within the field of the camera's view. Like Greta, they all smiled as they looked at me through the screen.

"No..." I said again, then my voice dissolved in a groan as a swell of sudden vertigo hit. I swayed unsteadily on my feet, clutching my chair to remain upright. All the strength seemed to have drained from my legs, and my face felt hot, my cheeks flushed and burning, my vision swimming in and out of focus.

The muffins. Had they drugged me with them? *Oh, God, no, no...*

"No..." I whispered, shaking my head. "No, please...you can't..."

"Anathema," Greta murmured, then ducked her head, pulling on a black leather plague mask. One by one, the others behind her followed suit, slipping plague masks on, all chanting "Anathema...anathema...anathema..."

We stopped you, I wanted to scream. *Rodriguez and I—we stopped all of this from happening!*

From the kitchen, I heard the patio door rattle in its tracks as it slid open, and heavy footsteps rushing across the living room floor. I turned in horror as they circled me: men in plague masks, gloved hands outstretched.

"No," I pleaded as they grabbed my arms, dragging me toward the front door. "No, goddamn it, no—!"

"Go to sleep, little baby," I heard Greta croon from the computer behind me, the other members of the Corvus Society joining in for the chorus:

*"When you wake, you'll have sweet cake,
And all the pretty little horses..."*

About the Author

S.E. Howard grew up in the heart of Kentucky, the Bluegrass state, and has worked as a newspaper reporter, travel writer, and magazine editor. Her horror short story, "You've Been Saved" was adapted for film in the 2022 independently produced anthology Worst Laid Plans by GenreBlast Films. Other horror titles include the novella Prairie Madness with Baynam Books Press, and her novel-length debut The Vessel with Wicked House Publishing,. Find out more at www.sehoward.com and www.facebook.com/sehoward.author.

WICKED HOUSE PUBLISHING

Come find us!

Amazon: Wicked House Publishing
Mailing List: Sign Up Here!
Facebook Group: The Wicked House Cult of Slightly Insane Readers

- facebook.com/WickedHousePublishing
- x.com/WickedHousePub
- instagram.com/wicked_house_publishing